MANILA NOIR

EDITED BY JESSICA HAGEDORN

Published by Akashic Books
©2013 Akashic Books
Copyright to the individual stories is retained by the authors

Series concept by Tim McLoughlin and Johnny Temple
Manila map by Aaron Petrovich

ISBN-13: 978-1-61775-160-8
Library of Congress Control Number: 2012954508
All rights reserved

First printing

Akashic Books
PO Box 1456
New York, NY 10009
info@akashicbooks.com
www.akashicbooks.com

ALSO IN THE AKASHIC BOOKS NOIR SERIES

BALTIMORE NOIR, edited by LAURA LIPPMAN

BARCELONA NOIR (SPAIN), edited by ADRIANA V. LÓPEZ & CARMEN OSPINA

BOSTON NOIR, edited by DENNIS LEHANE

BOSTON NOIR 2: THE CLASSICS, edited by DENNIS LEHANE, JAIME CLARKE & MARY COTTON

BRONX NOIR, edited by S.J. ROZAN

BROOKLYN NOIR, edited by TIM McLOUGHLIN

BROOKLYN NOIR 2: THE CLASSICS, edited by TIM McLOUGHLIN

BROOKLYN NOIR 3: NOTHING BUT THE TRUTH, edited by TIM McLOUGHLIN & THOMAS ADCOCK

CAPE COD NOIR, edited by DAVID L. ULIN

CHICAGO NOIR, edited by NEAL POLLACK

COPENHAGEN NOIR (DENMARK), edited by BO TAO MICHAËLIS

D.C. NOIR, edited by GEORGE PELECANOS

D.C. NOIR 2: THE CLASSICS, edited by GEORGE PELECANOS

DELHI NOIR (INDIA), edited by HIRSH SAWHNEY

DETROIT NOIR, edited by E.J. OLSEN & JOHN C. HOCKING

DUBLIN NOIR (IRELAND), edited by KEN BRUEN

HAITI NOIR, edited by EDWIDGE DANTICAT

HAVANA NOIR (CUBA), edited by ACHY OBEJAS

INDIAN COUNTRY NOIR, edited by SARAH CORTEZ & LIZ MARTÍNEZ

ISTANBUL NOIR (TURKEY), edited by MUSTAFA ZIYALAN & AMY SPANGLER

KANSAS CITY NOIR, edited by STEVE PAUL

KINGSTON NOIR (JAMAICA), edited by COLIN CHANNER

LAS VEGAS NOIR, edited by JARRET KEENE & TODD JAMES PIERCE

LONDON NOIR (ENGLAND), edited by CATHI UNSWORTH

LONE STAR NOIR, edited by BOBBY BYRD & JOHNNY BYRD

LONG ISLAND NOIR, edited by KAYLIE JONES

LOS ANGELES NOIR, edited by DENISE HAMILTON

LOS ANGELES NOIR 2: THE CLASSICS, edited by DENISE HAMILTON

MANHATTAN NOIR, edited by LAWRENCE BLOCK

MANHATTAN NOIR 2: THE CLASSICS, edited by LAWRENCE BLOCK

MEXICO CITY NOIR (MEXICO), edited by PACO I. TAIBO II

MIAMI NOIR, edited by LES STANDIFORD

MOSCOW NOIR (RUSSIA), edited by NATALIA SMIRNOVA & JULIA GOUMEN

MUMBAI NOIR (INDIA), edited by ALTAF TYREWALA

NEW JERSEY NOIR, edited by JOYCE CAROL OATES

NEW ORLEANS NOIR, edited by JULIE SMITH

ORANGE COUNTY NOIR, edited by GARY PHILLIPS

PARIS NOIR (FRANCE), edited by AURÉLIEN MASSON

PHILADELPHIA NOIR, edited by CARLIN ROMANO

PHOENIX NOIR, edited by PATRICK MILLIKIN

PITTSBURGH NOIR, edited by KATHLEEN GEORGE

PORTLAND NOIR, edited by KEVIN SAMPSELL

QUEENS NOIR, edited by ROBERT KNIGHTLY

RICHMOND NOIR, edited by ANDREW BLOSSOM, BRIAN CASTLEBERRY & TOM DE HAVEN

ROME NOIR (ITALY), edited by CHIARA STANGALINO & MAXIM JAKUBOWSKI

ST. PETERSBURG NOIR (RUSSIA), edited by NATALIA SMIRNOVA & JULIA GOUMEN

SAN DIEGO NOIR, edited by MARYELIZABETH HART

SAN FRANCISCO NOIR, edited by PETER MARAVELIS

SAN FRANCISCO NOIR 2: THE CLASSICS, edited by PETER MARAVELIS

SEATTLE NOIR, edited by CURT COLBERT

STATEN ISLAND NOIR, edited by PATRICIA SMITH

TORONTO NOIR (CANADA), edited by JANINE ARMIN & NATHANIEL G. MOORE

TRINIDAD NOIR (TRINIDAD & TOBAGO), edited by LISA ALLEN-AGOSTINI & JEANNE MASON

TWIN CITIES NOIR, edited by JULIE SCHAPER & STEVEN HORWITZ

VENICE NOIR (ITALY), edited by MAXIM JAKUBOWSKI

WALL STREET NOIR, edited by PETER SPIEGELMAN

FORTHCOMING

BAGHDAD NOIR (IRAQ), edited by SAMUEL SHIMON

BEIRUT NOIR (LEBANON), edited by IMAN HUMAYDAN

BOGOTÁ NOIR (COLOMBIA), edited by ANDREA MONTEJO

BUFFALO NOIR, edited by BRIGID HUGHES & ED PARK

DALLAS NOIR, edited by DAVID HALE SMITH

HAITI NOIR 2: THE CLASSICS, edited by EDWIDGE DANTICAT

HELSINKI NOIR (FINLAND), edited by JAMES THOMPSON

JERUSALEM NOIR, edited by DROR MISHANI

LAGOS NOIR (NIGERIA), edited by CHRIS ABANI

MISSISSIPPI NOIR, edited by TOM FRANKLIN

PRISON NOIR, edited by JOYCE CAROL OATES

SEOUL NOIR (KOREA), edited by BS PUBLISHING CO.

SINGAPORE NOIR, edited by CHERYL LU-LIEN TAN

TEL AVIV NOIR (ISRAEL), edited by ETGAR KERET & ASSAF GAVRON

USA NOIR, edited by JOHNNY TEMPLE

PHILIPPINES

Dingalan Bay

Lamon Bay

Manila

Laguna de Bay

Balayan
Bay

Tayabas Bay

South China Sea

Sibuyan Sea

Tablas Strait

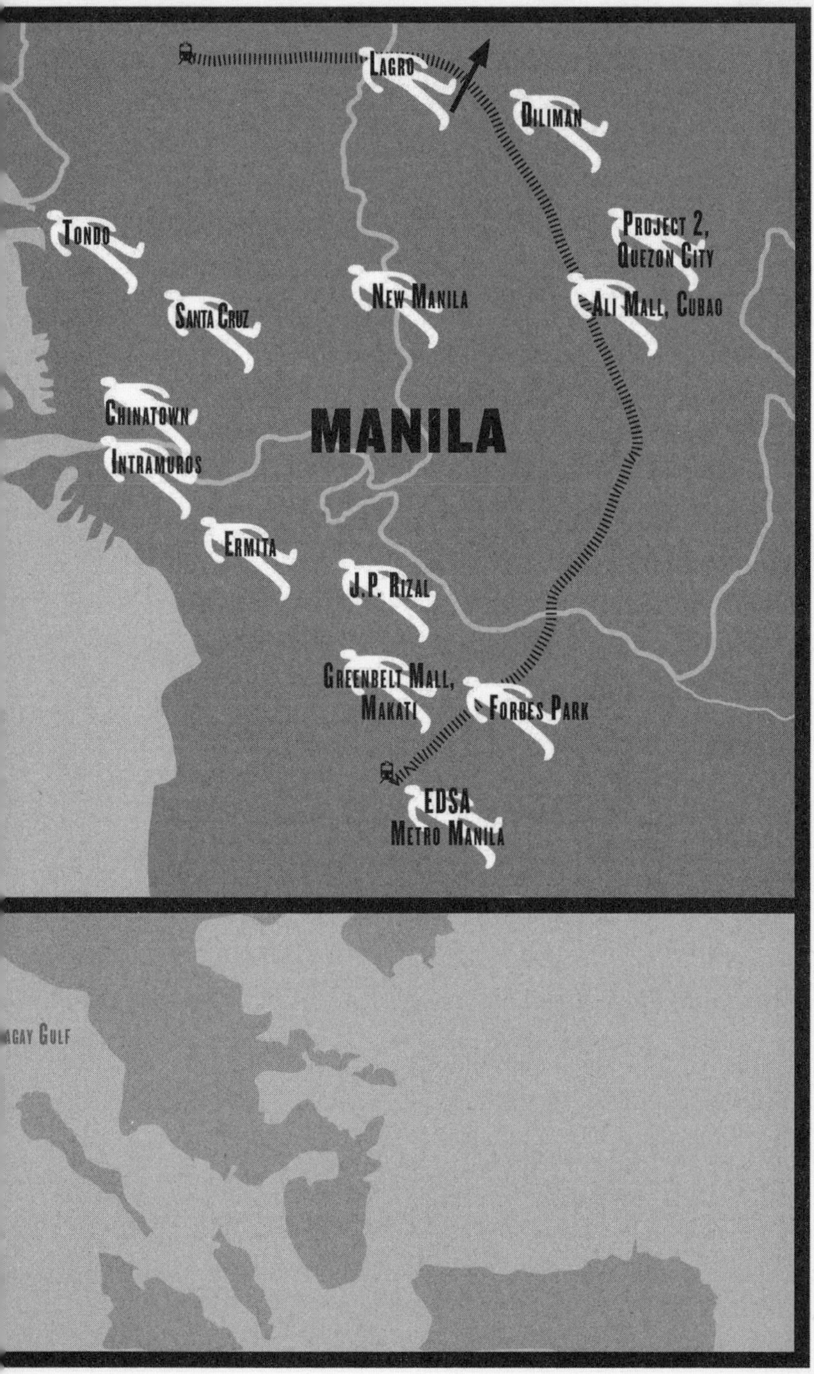

Lagro
Diliman
Tondo
Project 2, Quezon City
Santa Cruz
New Manila
Ali Mall, Cubao
Chinatown
MANILA
Intramuros
Ermita
J.P. Rizal
Greenbelt Mall, Makati
Forbes Park
EDSA
Metro Manila
agay Gulf

TABLE OF CONTENTS

PART III: THEY LIVE BY NIGHT

INTRODUCTION
Femme Fatale

1. She mostly wears red. And sometimes black.

I like to think of Manila as a woman of mystery, the ultimate femme fatale. Sexy, complicated, and tainted by a dark and painful past, she's not to be trusted. And why should she be? She's been betrayed time and again, invaded, plundered, raped, and pillaged, colonized for nearly four hundred years by Spain and fifty years by the United States, brutally occupied from 1942 to 1945 by the Japanese army, bombed and pretty much decimated by Japanese and US forces during an epic, month-long battle in 1945. In spite, or because of this bloody history, Manileños (her wild and wayward children) have managed to adapt, survive, and even thrive. Their ability to bounce back—whether from the latest round of catastrophic flooding, the ashes of a twenty-year dictatorship, or a horrific world war—never ceases to amaze.

Manila is where I was born, a city of heat and shadow and secrets, perfect for this genre we call noir. Built on water and reclaimed land, Manila has evolved over the years into an intense, congested, teeming megalopolis, the vital core of an urban network of sixteen cities and one municipality nowadays collectively known as Metro Manila. Around twelve million people live there presently, maybe more. The numbers are increasing by the minute.

Can we talk about her considerable nostalgic charm? Roxas Boulevard, a waterfront roadway along Manila Bay, is akin to the Malecón in old Havana, Cuba, down to its stately coconut palm trees, glorious sunsets, and fraught colonial history. The esplanade along the eroding seawall is one of Manila's few democratic public spaces. Where anyone, rich or poor, can seek respite from the clamor and pollution of the city and gaze at the water and dream. Both Roxas and Havana's Malecón were constructed during the early 1900s, when Cuba and the Philippines were under US military rule. When I was a child, Roxas was known as Dewey Boulevard, after the American admiral. Back then, I never questioned the weirdness of all those streets named after Americans; that tells you everything. The US embassy is still located on one end of Roxas Boulevard, to this day a site of hope, deep resentment, and longing. Under a boiling sun, Filipinos line up to apply for their exit visas. The lines are long. So is the wait.

2. Ghosts

Many Filipinos of a certain generation will remain forever haunted by the twenty-year reign of Ferdinand Marcos and his glamorous "Steel Butterfly" first lady, Imelda. Many would rather forget. After all, Ferdinand Marcos is dead. And his eighty-three-year-old widow, once-feared and reviled, now merely comes across as dotty and harmless. The Marcos regime was enthusiastically backed by the US from the start, until the plundering of coffers, the declaration of martial law, the widespread use of torture and killing of dissidents, and the brazen assassination of Senator Ninoy Aquino became much too embarrassing. The people stormed the palace, the Marcoses fled to Hawaii, and their corrupt rule came to a spectacular and very public end in 1986. Or did it?

In the Philippines, playful nicknames are ubiquitous and history has a way of repeating itself in the most ironic of ways. Ferdinand "Bong Bong" Marcos Jr., the only son of Ferdinand and Imelda, is now a senator. Benigno "Noynoy" Aquino III, whose mother was the iconic President Corazon Aquino and whose father was the equally iconic Senator Ninoy Aquino, is the current president. Dashing, handsome Ninoy happened to be one of Imelda's early suitors. It can get really confusing. Ninoy led the opposition against the Marcos government and was shot getting off the plane at Manila International Airport when he returned from exile in 1983. The assassination made headlines worldwide; Ninoy Aquino became a national hero and a martyr for the cause. The airport has been renamed after him. There's an official holiday and a museum. The mastermind behind Aquino's very public murder—whether it was Ferdy, Imelda, or some pissed-off army general or someone else—remains a mystery.

Many years have passed since the dark times of martial law and the Marcos dictatorship. People are now free to write and say what they want. The economy seems to be on an upswing. Call centers are big business, and there are art galleries, indie bands, and film collectives flourishing in places like Quezon City. But glaring inequities still exist, and workers must toil in faraway places like Saudi Arabia, Israel, Germany, Italy, Spain, and Iceland just to support their families. There have been many documented cases of female domestic overseas workers being treated as slaves, sexually and physically abused, even killed by their employers.

3. Either nothing surprises you in Manila, or everything does.
Here's a telling story. The current four-term mayor of Manila, Alfredo Lim, is a former senator and former cop. He's an avuncular kinda guy, known by his colorful moniker: Dirty Harry. One of his legendary stunts involved spray-painting the homes of alleged drug dealers in red. The people ate it up. Though the people aren't stupid—they just know a good stunt when they see one. In 2008, his forty-four-year-old "businessman" son Man-

uel was busted attempting to sell one hundred grams of *shabu* (crystal meth) to an undercover agent. You can go online and Google the whole sorry, sordid mess. Needless to say, the mayor played the part of the stern, glowering father. "He's forty-four years old," Mayor Lim said about his son's arrest in the *Philippine Daily Inquirer.* "He should be ready to face the consequences of his actions. Let him suffer . . ." Needless to say, witnesses for the prosecution never bothered showing up and the case was quickly thrown out of court. Fast-forward to 2012. Mayor Lim announces his plans to run for reelection in 2013. Challenging him will be former impeached president and mustachioed action star Joseph Estrada, once voted "the tenth most corrupt leader in the world." Ah, yes. Another day in the life.

4. *There are crimes, and there are* crimes.
Manila's a city of survivors, schemers, and dreamers. Where a down-and-out kid from the sticks named Manny Pacquiao can punch his way to the top with his fists, become a congressman, star in action movies, and—like other action stars before him— maybe even one day become president.

Manila's a city of extremes. Where the rich live in posh enclaves, guarded by men with guns. Where the poor improvise homes out of wood, tin, and cardboard and live by their wits. Where five-star hotels and luxury malls selling Prada and Louis Vuitton coexist with toxic garbage dumps and sprawling "informal settlements" (a.k.a. squatter settlements), where religious zeal coexists with superstition, where "hospitality" might be another word for prostitution, where sports and show business can be the first step to politics, where politics can be synonymous with nepotism, cronyism, and corruption, where violence is nothing out of the ordinary, and pretty much anything can be had for a price—if you have the money and/or the connections, that is.

The cops are often in collusion with the syndicates behind many of the more profitable crimes like kidnapping, extortion, human trafficking, and drugs. Justice is questionable. Homicides are often fueled by jealous rage, a thirst for revenge, machismo, and unrequited love. Or by a paranoid psychosis brought on by smoking *shabu*. Or maybe, just maybe, by hanging out in a karaoke dive, drinking too much, and singing "My Way" in the wrong key.

Writers from the Americas and Europe are known for a certain style of noir fiction, but the rest of the world approaches the crime story from culturally unique perspectives. The Philippines has produced many distinguished writers and poets writing in English. It's a shame that these works are so hard to come by outside of the Philippines. Several contemporary writers have left their indelible mark on crime fiction. Three immediately come to mind: Charlson Ong, F.H. Batacan, and Wilfredo Garrido. In putting this anthology together, I found the noir genre flexible enough to accommodate the Filipino flair for the gothic and the world of the supernatural. The modern Filipino can be urbane and cosmopolitan, wear delicate crosses and amulets around his or her neck, go to confession on Fridays, club-hop on Saturdays, and attend Mass on Sundays, while still believing in the presence of *duendes*, *kapres*, and bloodsucking *aswangs*. As you will see from this steamy collection of stories, all these delicious contradictions serve to enrich and expand our concept of noir. What you will also find are the noir essentials: alienated and desperate characters, terse dialogue, sudden violence, betrayals left and right. And of course, there's plenty of mordant humor. And of course, there are no happy endings.

5. Fabulous & Fearless
Gina Apostol, F.H. Batacan, Jose Dalisay, Lourd de Veyra, Eric Gamalinda, Angelo R. Lacuesta, R. Zamora Linmark, Rosario

Cruz-Lucero, Sabina Murray, Marianne Villanueva, Jonas Vit-man, Lysley Tenorio, and the graphic noir team of Budjette Tan and Kajo Baldisimo serve up a real taste of life in one of the wildest cities on the planet. The characters and locations are all over the map in the best possible way. There are transves-tites and transsexuals in Chinatown and Tondo, shabuheads in Quezon City, feral street kids in Makati, lovelorn professors in Diliman, and even a Jesuit forensic anthropologist investigating a murder in Lagro. The surprise centerpiece of this anthology is Tan & Baldisimo's "Thirteen Stations," a graphic noir set in public transit stations where ghastly crimes are taking place. Cool, otherworldly detective Alexandra Trese, the heroine of Tan & Baldisimo's hugely popular *Trese* series, is summoned to deal with these crimes. It made perfect sense to include a graphic noir, since one of the many ways I learned to become a writer was through the Filipino horror *komiks* of my childhood. Con-sider it my homage. All the fabulous and fearless writers gathered here, whether they are living in Manila, the US, or elsewhere in the ever-growing Philippine diaspora, have a deep connection and abiding love for this crazy-making, intoxicating city. There's nothing like it in the world, and they know it.

Jessica Hagedorn
March 2013

PART I

Us Against Them

AVIARY

BY LYSLEY TENORIO

Greenbelt Mall, Makati

When we learn about the sign, we must see it for our-selves. So from our shanties we cross the railway tracks and charge toward the home of Alejandro, the only kid we know with a computer, the only kid we know with *electricity*, so that he can show us a picture of the sign on the Internet. He lives with his mother in the Financial District now, in a big-shot, high-rise condominium which, he has said, overlooks the world. But it's not so high that we can't reach it: Alejandro calls the front desk to give us clearance, despite the security guard's suspicions, so we file into the elevator, rising and rising to the uppermost floors. When we reach his door, it's al-ready open, and he stands there waiting. "I'll show you on my computer," he says, "but don't touch the keyboard. Don't touch *anything*." He inspects our hands to make sure they're clean, then herds us into his bedroom. He flips open his laptop, types and clicks and types and clicks, until an image downloads, a pic-ture of a sign posted on a shopping mall door. It says:

THIS IS A PRIVATE, CONTROLLED ENVIRONMENT.
POOR PEOPLE & OTHER DISTURBING
REALITIES STRICTLY PROHIBITED.
THANK YOU!
GREENBELT MALL

"So the story is true," says Alejandro, closing his laptop, "they really don't want you there." He half-smiles at us and shrugs, a funny story to him but an injustice to us, so we curse its name and unleash all the profanity we know: *Fuck you Greenbelt Mall, you asshole Greenbelt Mall, shit bitch motherfucker go to hell Greenbelt Mall.*

Greenbelt Mall is mere kilometers from our part of Makati City. From certain vantage points and heights, we have witnessed its nighttime glow of green and red during past Christmas seasons, and we have heard the blare of marching bands that celebrate every grand opening and ribbon-cutting ceremony. But have we been inside? No way! We have no use for Tokyo-inspired fur and leather winter coats. We don't want imported and indigestible cheeses. Our lives are made no better by facial cleansers made from organic jackfruit and nuts. And say we did go there one day, say we purchased even the smallest trinket like a souvenir Greenbelt key chain or a stylish Greenbelt visor. We would be called arrogant big-shots who think we're hot shit. People trying to be other people.

But we will not be prohibited from entering. We will not allow ourselves to be banned. We decide then and there to act, to right this terrible wrong.

"And do what? Get revenge?" Alejandro laughs, but we don't.

The front door rattles open. "My mom's home," Alejandro says. "Leave." He scoots us from his room, and on our way out we see his mother staring out a wall of windows at a view of skyscrapers, palm trees, a grid of streets that from here look orderly and clean. She is wearing a dress as black and tight as a silhouette, holds a long brown cigarette in one hand and an amber-colored drink with clinking ice in the other. She is the blondest Filipina we have ever seen, and her face is half-gone behind dark glasses, huge and round like two black moons.

With a long red fingernail, she lowers her sunglasses, looks us up and down with recognition and suspicion, as though we remind her of what she comes from.

We look around her, at this roomful of things we will never have—a white leather sofa and a rug of white fur, a dining table with elephant tusk legs, a strong ceiling free of cracks and leaks, and an equally sturdy floor. But our envy is tempered by our pity. We know the things she does to live this life. We have seen her strolling down the street on the arms of businessmen—Japanese, Indian, Saudi Arabian, American—and we know there are nights when Alejandro must find somewhere else to sleep, and on those nights he comes to us.

"Get out," she says.

We exit, enter the elevator, feel our descent.

It's dusk by the time we're home, and Auntie Fritzie is already scolding us as we come into view. In her yellow poncho and pink rubber boots, she has been scavenging through the dumps and trash heaps, and has lined up her findings in messy piles along the railway track. She tells us to hurry our lazy asses and get to work, says that if our mothers and fathers were alive, they would smack our faces for our laziness. So we sort through tattered shoes, sticky soda bottles, chipped plates, flicking away the things that cling to them. Toiling through muck and stench, we keep on cursing Greenbelt Mall, daydreaming of the revenge Alejandro spoke of, and the many ways to get it.

This morning, we don black. Polo shirts and corduroys, our only good clothes, the outfits we wear to baptisms and funerals. We grab backpacks and slip on dark glasses, intact pairs collected from the years of Auntie Fritzie's scavenging, and as we make our way to the center of Makati City, they turn the gray day grayer.

1, 2, 3, 4, 5: Greenbelt Mall is made of five interconnected buildings, 4 and 5 the most elite, the ones that aim to keep us out. We walk toward the main entrance of Greenbelt 4, a fortress of a structure surrounded by colossal palm trees and twisty moatlike fountains, with glass awnings jutting toward the sky.

We arrive at a set of double glass doors. Inside, on a marble pillar, hangs the sign we saw the day before. We step forward. The doors whoosh open. We're in.

Greenbelt air is cold, the coldest air ever, and why are the shoppers' faces so narrow and pointy and white? Back and forth across the shiny rows of shiny stores, up and down the escalators, these are the whitest Filipinos we have ever seen. No one regards us when we pass, as if we are the ghostly ones, not them.

We don't know where to go, not at first, so we follow a group of teenaged girls not much older than us. We whistle at them, make catcalls, and though they keep their distance we stay close, and finally they lead us to a store whose name we have seen before but never said aloud—Louis Vuitton. The girls walk through the doors, but we stop just short of them, surveying the scene inside: skinny men with slicked-back hair stand behind long display cases full of leather bags and wallets, some so special they require their own glass encasement; women coo over them, like nurses in a room full of newborn babies. Light comes from every corner, giving the entire store a butter-colored glow, and when we finally step inside, we seem to light up too.

One of the skinny men, safe behind a row of leather briefcases, welcomes us with a meaningless nod. A woman who could be his twin sister approaches, heels clacking against the floor like a ticking clock. "Can I help you?" she asks.

We shake our heads no.

"Is there nothing I can help you find?" she asks. It may be a trick question; her eyes shift toward the security guard standing by the door.

We tell her we're looking for a present, something special for our aunt, and before she can offer phony customer service we disperse, spread ourselves throughout the store, upstairs to the Men's Universe, downstairs to the Women's Universe, and we even infiltrate a room called the Private Salon, where two of the skinny men show a set of leather wallets to an old woman sitting in the middle of a three-person sofa, a teacup in her hand. The skinny men look up, their faces full of dismay. "Can I help you?" they ask together, but it's the old woman who tells us to leave. In another reality, Auntie Fritzie would be this woman on the sofa. Though she scolds, belittles, and hits us constantly, it would be nice to see her sitting in something pillowy and warm. Such a moment might soften her; perhaps she would be easier for us to please.

"I said leave," the woman repeats.

We do not move, not for several moments. Not until we're ready.

Finally, we go.

We exit the Private Salon, return to the main floor. We gather at a corner display of what a sign calls "weekend bags." They are leather bags with long leather straps, with buttons, buckles, and rivets, all gold, everywhere. The price of even the smallest ones startles us. We have no idea what that kind of money could buy, how much of it, but the possibilities seem endless.

A few of us walk to the front of the store, pretend to accidentally knock over a rack of coin purses. Diversion created, the rest of us unzip our satchels and pull out plastic bags containing the bodies of small dead birds. We had heard that an aviary once stood on the land Greenbelt occupies now; imagine all those homeless birds, how they aimlessly flew, how swiftly

...ey perished. Where we live, dead birds are everywhere: on the ground and in mounds of trash; they even make their way, somehow, into Auntie Fritzie's daily collections. The bodies are ashen, gray with death, dirt, dried-up blood, and exposed organs. Some crawl with fleas and lice. Carefully, without touching them, we drop a bird into the smallest compartment of each travel bag, one by one by one. When we finish, we slip out of the store, as easily as we entered.

We walk away twenty paces, then turn back toward Louis Vuitton. We imagine the people who will find these birds, how they will first mistake them for balls of thread or yarn, wads of unexpected dust. But when they look closer, they will blink several times, shudder, then scream at the thing they hold in their hands.

We leave Louis Vuitton behind, continue through Greenbelt 4, passing stores with nonsensical names—BVLGARI, BOTTEGA VENETTA—and others that sound like a sneeze—GUCCI, Jimmy Choo. Whole families drift in and out of them—what small boy needs Norwegian perfume? What stink could he possibly possess to require so expensive a scent? We might be angered if we weren't so baffled, so for a time we simply ride the escalators and observe the wastefulness all around us. We ride up, we ride down, over and over, and sometimes glimpse ourselves in the mall's many mirrored surfaces. In certain moments, one wall reflects another, multiplying us as we ascend and descend, ascend and descend, as if there are hundreds of us, maybe thousands, seemingly everywhere, going nowhere.

From Greenbelt 4 we go to 5. On an empty bench we find a promotional pamphlet, with a customer testimonial that says, *Greenbelt 5—it's like you're not in the Philippines!* We crumple it up, toss it in the trash, then peer through a storefront window and watch a white-faced Filipino couple purchase jewel-tipped shoes and a gold-framed oil painting in the same transaction, while their small daughters play games and send text messages on their hi-tech phones. We leave this scene and walk down a row of stores, then stop at one we recognize, Kenneth Cole, because Auntie Fritzie once found a barely scuffed coin purse bearing a tag with the same name, a prized possession even now. But their window displays perturb us: each features a group of silver mannequins dressed in black and gray evening wear, some lounging about in twisty wire chairs, other posed to look as if they are in midconversation. But they're all headless, and we don't understand this. So we step inside the near-empty store, and find a tiny-bodied salesgirl folding black satin shirts into perfect rectangles. She looks up, startled. "Can I help you?" she asks, a question we are already so tired of, but this time we say yes, and we ask: Where are the heads? What did she or her manager or Kenneth Cole himself do with them, and why are they not connected to their bodies? She blinks, shakes her head, says, "Excuse me?" We repeat our questions and she answers, "You need to leave." We do not. Instead, we come closer, catching sight of ourselves in the concave security mirror in the upper corner of the ceiling: a circle of black figures surrounding one small girl, closing in, no chance of escape. Does she know how often we feel this way, between our cardboard walls, beneath our low corrugated roofs? Does she understand?

"Please go," she says.

We are done here, so one by one we uncircle the girl, exit Kenneth Cole single file, and en route to the door we clear our throats and spit out loogies on a row of leather gloves displayed palms up.

We charge through the rest of Greenbelt 5, entering and exiting any store we choose. Our presence baffles every salesman and woman; we never make our intentions clear. In Banana Republic, we stand in a line, trying on the same safari jacket one at a time, then leave it rumpled on the floor. In Prizmic & Brill, we take turns sitting on every chair for sale, but quickly, so as not to become too comfortable. We insert ourselves among the crowd of pregnant women inside Havin' a Baby, then gather around an empty white cradle, which we rock back and forth as we remember dead babies we have known. At Spex, we ignore the glasses on display and simply look at ourselves in the lit-up mirrors, the mysteriousness of our dark glasses, our facelessness beneath. Then, when we pass Rolex, we pay our respects: not long before, a group of armed men robbed the store, smashing and smashing with the ends of their guns every glass case of watches. Most escaped, but one was shot dead by Greenbelt security. The news reports said he was someone like us, a man who tried to change his life. We imagine him splayed on the store's doorstep, his blood congealing on the ground beneath his dying body.

In front of Rolex, we gather in a circle. We have a moment of silence, then one of us takes out a razor blade, gives a quick slash to his palm, lets blood drip onto the mall's marble floor.

A samurai raises his sword over two lovers slurping thick, wormy noodles from a steaming white bowl. We half wish it was real, that the samurai could come to life and lop off the heads of these diners. But the samurai is just a character in a movie projected on the wall of a restaurant called johnandyoko, a name as strange as the food they serve—slivers of raw fish that look like tongues, piled high on top of each other, and surrounded with leaves and dots of orange and magenta sauce, on dinner plates so large they're mostly empty. We cannot fathom becoming full off such small food, but as we stand here, lined up along the window and staring in, the diners seem to delight in the tininess of their meals.

We lick our fingers and draw X's on the window glass, over the diners' faces. We do the same at other elegant restaurants in Greenbelt 5—The Terrace, Chateau 1771, Chili's—watching up close the people inside, crossing them out. Strange as their food is, we can't deny the fact that we had no breakfast, but we fend off hunger by telling ourselves that we aren't wanted here, and even if they offered us a sample, just a small quick taste, we would never eat it.

We've breathed enough of the Greenbelt air. We exit through one of the many entrances, find ourselves in a cool and breezy courtyard, where parents lounge on blankets laid out on the grass, as their giggling children run circles around them. We stop to stare at some of them, and move on.

Then we see it, there in the distance: a domelike structure resembling the top half of a UFO. We move toward it slowly, cautiously, as if it might take flight at any moment. And then we discover that the building is the Greenbelt Chapel. A place for worship between shopping; we are not impressed. Still, there are no signs prohibiting our entry.

We enter with no intentions. Then we are amazed.

We have never seen anything so wondrous, such unearthly beauty. Every wall and panel curves around, swoops up from the ground and meets at the top, where a stained-glass Jesus Christ surrounded by golden light gazes down upon us. At the other end of the chapel, choir members gather, practicing the first notes of some holy song. So humbled are we by this magnificence that we remove our dark glasses, file into a pew, and drop to our knees. Terrible storms leveled off our church long ago; for years we have worshipped alongside the empty railway tracks, in the heat and in the cold, which, we realize now, has made it difficult to pray. But in this mostly empty church, we fall easily into prayer. Our heads bowed, we are so silent we can hear the sound of our own breathing, somehow in rhythm with the choir's song.

In the name of the Father, the Son, and the Holy Spirit, Amen.

We raise our heads, and then we see it, a shock of blond hair at the end of the pew of the very first row. Alejandro's mother. She crosses herself then stands up, still in her black dress and dark glasses. She picks up a pair of shopping bags by her feet, walks slowly up the aisle. We bow our heads again, hoping to remain unseen.

She stops at the end of our row, lowers her sunglasses, revealing a bruised black eye. She looks us over, one face at a time. "You don't belong here," she whispers, in a tone that sounds like wisdom. Then she looks away at something behind us. We turn and see what she sees: family after family arriving for Mass, whole generations, all in flawless clothing, perfectly shined shoes. Alejandro's mother moves on, and then we notice a man in a navy-blue suit with gold buttons, the father of what looks to be a prominent family, staring at us from across the aisle, whispering to a woman who may be his wife, and our good clothes now look meager, the holes and frays of our shirts more noticeable than before.

We don our dark glasses. It's time for us to leave.

But first, we decide that this is the spot, the place we will leave our final mark. From one of our satchels we remove—carefully, delicately—a segment of metal pipe wrapped with blue and red wire, with a cell phone duct-taped to it. We place it under the pew before us, right in the middle, where someone whose head is bowed in prayer but not truly praying might notice it, if he or she looks closely enough.

We stand and walk out of the Greenbelt Chapel, make our way home.

It will not detonate. Fake things never do. Instead of explosions there will be mass panic and hysteria, which we will read about in discarded newspapers, or on the Internet, if Alejandro will let us onto his computer again. The Greenbelt Mall authorities will call it a hoax, a false alarm; they will promise the people there is nothing to fear. Still, the damage will be done. We will have created unease here, severe emotional distress, a disturbance they will not soon forget. And when they do, we will strike again, in ways we ourselves have yet to know.

A HUMAN RIGHT

BY ROSARIO CRUZ-LUCERO

Intramuros

C asa Manila," the docent announces, pushing the massive double doors twice before they give way. His memorized spiels are in impeccable, if textbook English. "Notice the furniture and appurtenances." The nervous young thing is obviously new to this job, though Isabel would guess, by his robotic accent and tone, that he's had a stint as a call center agent. But the quaintness of his jargon keeps with the whole design of Intramuros, the walled "city within the city."

Isabel smiles at him encouragingly and he smiles back.

"This replica of a nineteenth-century Hispanic house was actually built in 1979."

Ah, Isabel thinks, another of Imelda Marcos's "cultural projects," meaning the epitome of kitsch.

". . . Spanish-Filipino baroque," he continues. "The antique furniture and trappings that fill up these capacious rooms are authentic and collected from other houses."

"Confiscated, you mean," says a pudgy, dark-skinned little man. He looks every inch Filipino, but speaks with a drawl from the American South that seems to hang between Liverpool and Boracay. One of those who'd fled the country, Isabel concludes, at the height of the Marcos dictatorship. And still bitter about it.

Isabel detaches herself from the group and walks ahead to the next room. It's enormous, and she is delighted to see that there is an open window taking up the whole length of the space.

In broad daylight, this would be the cheeriest room in the house, but the late-afternoon sun has cast shadows on the pillars and walls.

Isabel gazes out the window and discovers that she is actually facing out the back of the house. With all the large doors, the room partitions, the mirrors, she hadn't realized till now that she'd lost her bearings. From this window, she sees, across the gray roofs, Intramuros's ramparts, with a watchtower at one end and a sentry box at the other. Across the faux-cobblestone road is the mass of shanties known as Barrio Santa Lucia.

Informal settlers. Slum dwellers have their own euphemism too, Isabel thinks in amusement. One more exhibit for the tourists of Intramuros, who can see the cross-section of Manila life without the muck and stench and, most of all, the dangers.

A man stands at the entrance to the shantytown. Isabel leans forward to take a closer look—the man's profile is distinctive: the high forehead, the sharp cheekbones, the corner of the mouth sloping downward so that it gives him a perpetually somber look, the curly black hair growing close to the scalp.

"Elias," Isabel mutters under her breath. A scar cutting an eyebrow would make her more certain, but she can't see it clearly from this distance.

He suddenly glances up, as if he has heard her thoughts. He continues staring, with that familiar somber expression she remembers from—how long has it been?—eighteen years ago. Isabel jerks away from the window. Not nervously, nor surreptitiously, but because the docent's voice has startled her back to her surroundings.

It's five o'clock, the docent says. Closing time. Only then does Isabel notice that the Casa Manila has gone all quiet.

She hurries out, hoping to find the man she thinks is Elias. A motorcycle engine zooms somewhere to her right and a horse pulling a *calesa* clip-clops to her left. She peers into the alley leading toward the barrio, but inside it's pitch-black, the crush of shanties perpetually shutting out the sun. She guesses the people who reside there are used to living in the dark.

Elias is gone, of course. Elias, her father's killer.

It couldn't possibly have been Elias, of course it couldn't, Isabel had protested at first, that day ten years ago back in Davao. Her mother had handed her the police report and declared flatly, "It was a DDS execution. And it was Elias who did it."

Señor and Señora Jose Fabella, the report read, were getting out of their car in front of their residence when a lone gunman on a Honda Wave motorcycle had stopped two meters away and shot Señor Fabella several times, first in the side, then in the neck, twice in the head—in the middle of the forehead and in the right cheek—and then in the chest. Then the gunman took off. Señora Fabella, who was stepping out curbside, and the family driver, who was helping her, were left unharmed.

The police were sure the killer was Elias Raga, a.k.a. the Datu. The MO was that of the Davao Death Squad, or the DDS, of which the Datu was a well-known but elusive leader. One of the Fabellas' servants had peered through the window when the shots rang out, and later told the cops that the gunman was wearing jeans and a black jacket; a baseball cap was pulled low over his eyes. The generic look of DDS killers. But what pointed to Elias as the prime and only suspect was that he knew more about the victim than any other DDS member. He had lived in the Fabella home for a few months at the age of thirteen. He knew Señor Fabella's routine. And he was familiar enough with the gated Village to know how to get in and out of it without arousing suspicion.

Despite its humble name, the Village, where Isabel and her

family lived, was the enclave of Davao's richest families. There were about a hundred mansions, guarded by a private army that made regular rounds and kept strict tabs on every car, bike, and pedestrian entering and exiting through its steel gates. A church, a park, a school, tennis and basketball courts, and a swimming pool—all for the exclusive use of its residents—made up its hub. A thick cement wall ran along the Village's whole perimeter, with glass shards embedded along its top.

The police report went on: Regrettably, none of the Village guards could be of any help in identifying the culprit. They had all vanished by the time the investigators had come—whether from fear of reprisal for their criminal negligence or fear of DDS execution if they testified was anyone's guess. Or, it was just as likely that the Village guards were themselves in cahoots with the DDS. Anything, the report concluded, was possible.

It was the classic conclusion to any case involving the DDS.

Isabel didn't believe it at first, not the part about her father's brutal murder being a DDS execution. Everyone knew that the DDS was a vigilante group that targeted young delinquents—only small-scale drug dealers and petty thieves. But her father was a respectable member of the Davao community and in his midfifties when he was shot. And DDS killers always operated in twos, sometimes threes. This had been a solo operation. Yet Isabel finally had to concede that the killer might have been—probably was—Elias the Datu, DDS leader, carrying out his own personal mission.

While the DDS were killers, they did set limits; it was a sort of code of honor, and by breaking it, the Datu had turned himself into a DDS target. Everyone knew that too. Now Elias was on the run.

Señor Fabella's coffin remained closed throughout the three-day wake and funeral. The widow wept intermittently during the wake and broke into a long wail as the coffin was lowered in the grave. No one saw Isabel weep.

More people are gathering in the streets now. There is a bustle of activity, the buzz of voices, the zooming of motorized tricycles. But the noises are more muted here than they would be in Extramuros, the real city just beyond the fortress walls. There seems to be a tacit agreement among everyone who comes here that this strained replica of nineteenth-century Spanish Manila should not only be respected but protected, because it is so brittle.

Most of the buildings here have been turned into offices or schools, so hardly anyone is a permanent resident in Intramuros anymore. Except the informal settlers. And the priests who run the churches, of which there are only two remaining, after American warplanes decimated this walled city with aerial bombs more than sixty years ago.

Just beside the slum is a school for seamen—seafarers, Isabel's editor would assiduously write over her copy, because in their line of work, being precise, he would remind her, is a matter of life and death. The students are coming out in waves, a few pausing at the top of the stairs to light a cigarette, barring the way for the others behind them.

A woman emerges from the barrio's dark alley. Isabel wonders if she is one of those who make a living at night. She wears a flowery dress, showing more of her slim legs than most Filipinas her age would dare, the area around her eyes painted with black and purple shadows, and her fuchsia lipstick spilling over the natural line of her lips to achieve the bee-stung look. She walks toward the school, where the young men are milling around outside.

Isabel thinks maybe this is the kind of woman who her husband—ex-husband, she corrects herself—had wanted her to be when he'd complained that sex with her was like thumbing through an encyclopedia—not just a volume of it, but a whole set. (A man with brains would find that exciting, she'd wanted to reply, but she was still trying to save the marriage then.)

The woman is now in the midst of the young men, who quickly part to get out of her arm's reach, some scurrying back a few steps up the stairs again, the rest hopping off the curb onto the street. Still, they are more respectful than one would expect, because they aren't hooting or heckling her. Instead they call out, "Hello, Ana!" and, "Nice dress, Ana!" She puts one hand on her hip and flicks her other at the men in dignified delight.

She is taller than all of them, even if she were to take off her shoes with the stiletto heels. She crosses the street toward Isabel, who is now pretending to read the Intramuros guidebook. Clearly the person named Ana relishes all the attention, because she could've crossed the street as soon as she'd emerged from the slum, instead of walking toward the young men first. It isn't until she stops barely a foot away from Isabel to adjust her bra-line that Isabel notices the shadow beneath the thick makeup.

"Hi," Isabel says, smiling, curious to hear the woman's voice.

"Hello," comes the husky reply. Ah.

Isabel was ten when Señora Fabella had come home from her charity work at the penal colony with Elias and his mother in tow. Elias's father had been serving out a life sentence, which had been cut short by a bullet in the head. A guard, the local paper said, had mistaken him for a wild boar that had wandered into the inmates' farm lots. Elias and his mother had been staying in the family quarters in the prison compound but now had nowhere to live. "The woman's a good cook," the prison chaplain had said to Señora Fabella. "And the boy's no trouble. Quiet. Small for his age. Thirteen. But very bright."

After a few minutes' resistance and his wife's gentle persuasion, Señor Fabella decided to give Elias and his mother a trial run. "A month in the plantation," he said to his wife, in their presence. "These Bagobo natives are the most treacherous tribe of all. Prone to criminal behavior, like the name suggests."

He would share his real misgivings with his wife later, in the privacy of their room. "For all you know, that Bagobo could've actually provoked the shooting," Señor Fabella said to his astonished wife. "He was a tribal chief, remember. The woman looks all right—she seems meek enough. But the boy!" Señor Fabella shook his head. "That's Bagobo blood running in his veins right there."

Yet Señor Fabella enjoyed playing both sides. After all, he'd be proven right either way. "You see?" he'd say. "I knew it wouldn't work." Or if it went the opposite way, he could say, "You see? I knew there was something beneath the obvious."

Isabel decides that there's still enough light for her to take a walking tour of Intramuros by herself. The guidebook has a fold-out map in it which she had studied the night before, after she'd checked in at the Intramuros Hotel. She has highlighted the places she wants to see on the map in orange and green neon. She has also highlighted the numbered items in the legend on the bottom half of the map with the same colors.

Elias used to tease Isabel about her obsessive reliance on maps. "Look, just follow the pathways—they also divide the fields from each other," he had said impatiently that summer eighteen years ago. Isabel was spending her long break from school on the family plantation, an hour's drive from Davao City. She had brought the map of their sixty-hectare plantation because she wanted to explore it herself, this time without her father by her side. Now she was turning it around, trying to match Banana Field 27 on the map with the real one.

Her father was grateful that Isabel showed such interest in the plantation; not every daughter did so. But her mother sent Elias after her anyway, just in case she got lost or needed anything, though Elias didn't tell Isabel this. Instead he ran after her, calling, "Hey, let me come with you."

"The fields all look the same," she said, bewildered. "They're all uniformly square."

"Yes, they are," Elias said, "and you don't need a map to tell you that."

"But this one," Isabel waved her hand at the banana trees closest to them, "how come this field doesn't match the shape of the one on the map? Look."

"It's nothing but a piece of paper with a lot of lines." Elias took the map from Isabel, folded it, and laid the paper in the middle of the footpath, then placed a rock over it. "We'll pick it up on our way back. C'mon, race you." With a whoop, he went running toward the hill that marked the edge of the field. Isabel sprinted after him. She couldn't have understood, because she didn't know, his exhilaration at being able to run in such wide-open space.

Within a month at the rural plantation, Señora Fabella was chafing to get back to her charity work in Davao City. Elias, too, had passed Señor Fabella's stipulated trial run. He was packed off to Davao with Isabel and her mother.

It was Sardo, the family driver, who first took to calling Elias "Datu." He'd say, "Hey, Datu, c'mere and help me wash the cars."

They'd been doing just that one morning when Sardo asked, "So, what were you in prison for?"

"I wasn't in prison," Elias replied. He rubbed a speck of bird dropping off the windshield and stepped back to study his handiwork. Sardo had stopped wiping down his half of the car and stood waiting. Elias realized he might have to do the Fabellas' whole fleet of cars by himself if he didn't elaborate. "It was a penal *farm*. We weren't behind bars or anything. My father had special privileges. My mother and I were allowed to live there with him, in the family quarters. And each family had a farm lot, so we could grow some cash crops." He didn't add that farm lots were for those who were there for the long haul.

"Okay," said Sardo, hunkering down to start with the tires. "So, what was your father in the penal farm for?"

"He and his people were carrying spears and blowpipes that happened to get in the way of landgrabbers and their private army. And my father was the datu—the chief. What would you call that crime?"

Sardo looked up from his scrubbing. He wasn't sure if Elias was joking; but then Elias had never struck him as a joker. "Illegal possession of deadly weapons?" he suggested. "Conspiracy to commit murder?" At last all those episodes of *Law & Order* and its spin-offs were paying dividends.

Elias smiled. "Rebellion. We're IPs—indigenous people. That's why we were in the penal farm, not jail."

"Oh well, that's all over now. Señor and Señora were talking about you yesterday, in the car. They're sending you to school, all the way to college. No point letting your brain go to waste washing cars, the señor said."

"Sure." Elias wrung water out of his rag. "So that one day he'll make me the head banana of the Fabella plantation. All this—" he indicated the Village with a sweep of his arm "—was Bagobo land, you know. This was *our* forest, all the way to the foot of the mountain. And then your masters came and stole it all with a piece of paper."

Sardo looked around cautiously, although Elias had spoken in a soft, even tone. "That was a long time ago. They were kind enough to take you in. Be grateful for that."

* * *

They didn't know yet then that in another month Elias would be gone.

It happened on a Saturday. Isabel came home from reading in the park and the servants were chattering excitedly in the kitchen. "What's going on?" Isabel asked.

"Someone took the money from the secret drawer underneath the altar of the Sacred Heart of Jesus," the housekeeper, who was the *mayor-doma*, answered. The mayor-doma had discovered the theft, because she was in charge of household expenses. Her voice rose shrilly: "I've worked for Señora Fabella longer than any of these other servants, and nothing like this has ever happened before."

"Don't worry, *manang*," the upstairs cleaning maid said. "We're all Christians here. Only a pagan would've stolen that money right under the eyes of the Lord Jesus."

The downstairs cleaning maid had the tact to nudge her with an elbow and shake her head in warning. Elias's mother was cooking lunch at the stove and could hear what they were saying, though they could not see her face.

Isabel left the kitchen to look for her mother. Señora Fabella was sitting on the patio, gazing forlornly at the garden. She told Isabel the rest of the story, the part that the servants didn't know about. "Your father called Elias into the master bedroom." When she saw the look on Isabel's face, Señora Fabella quickly added, "Just to question him about the missing money. But Elias refused to admit to the theft." She shook her head and passed her hand over her eyes. "One hundred pesos, taken from a sheaf of hundred-peso bills held together by a money-band. Elias—or whoever—didn't take it all. All Elias had to do was admit to stealing the hundred pesos."

"But he wouldn't," Isabel said.

Señora Fabella gazed at her daughter. "No, he wouldn't. He just stood there with his jaw clamped shut. Then your father asked me to leave the room, saying it was now a matter between two men. Minutes later, Elias came running out with a bloody cut on his eyebrow." Señora Fabella sighed. "Now I have to deal with the boy's mother." Then she added, "I hate it when your father is always proven right."

Isabel sat on the stool in front of her mother, a bag of books pressed close to her chest. There'd been a book stall at the park, selling discarded library books from American high schools at only twenty pesos each. "Mama," Isabel began, but couldn't go on.

Señora Fabella glanced at her daughter, then at the bulging bag. "Oh Isabel," she began, before falling silent. Isabel waited. Then Señora Fabella took a deep breath and repeated what her husband had said to her an hour before: "We will not speak of this again."

Isabel went to their secret cave later that day, sneaking out at siesta time—and the next day, and for days after that. It was Elias who had found the hole in the banyan tree behind the city hall, when he moved the rock covering it. It was big and deep enough for a small person to hide in. Here she left Elias sardine cans, only one or two a week, to avoid suspicion. She was ecstatic to find the cans gone every time she returned, and she went to bed knowing that Elias was safe in their secret cave, where he made his home every night. Isabel was convinced that if she found Elias, she would take him back home and confess the truth. But of what use was her confession if Elias wasn't there to be exonerated?

For six months she faithfully left him his sardines until, one morning, a box of imported Spam was delivered to the house. Señora Fabella rewarded the workers with bonus gifts of Spam each time they reaped a windfall at the plantation. That morning, Isabel slipped a can into her schoolbag and left it in the tree on her way home. The next day, after school, as she crossed the plaza to go to the tree with the hole, she saw a ragged old man sitting on the grass, clutching the can of imported Spam. He flashed her a toothless grin.

Soon, the words *The Datu*, scrawled over the zigzag figure of a crocodile, began to dominate Davao City's graffiti. The Datu's rise to street gang leadership was easy and quick. Cell phone snatching, not breaking-and-entering, was his specialty. But the Davao Death Squad's mission was to rid the city of vermin like him, either by extermination or recruitment. The Datu had all the makings of an excellent young recruit.

୨

The Philippine Center for Human Rights Research is a nongovernmental organization that monitors violations of human rights in the Philippines. It is committed to producing material that is well informed and objective. I am writing to solicit your views for our research on the pattern of execution-style killings of suspected petty criminals and street children.

Isabel glances up from her laptop to mull over the next sentence of her letter. Only then does she realize that the café in the Intramuros Hotel is now filled with people. She had been the only customer an hour ago, after strolling back from the Casa Manila. Next to her, there are two other people hunched over their laptops. Three ebony-haired elderly ladies are at another table, conversing softly. The quiet is unusual for a café these days, when such places have become the favorite venue for conducting job interviews or presenting sales pitches, interrupted only by the noise of motorcycle engines outside and the occasional backfire.

Isabel leans back in her chair and wishes, at this moment, that she had a more normal job than writing up reports on human rights violations. She's been stonewalled by enough government officials in her own hometown to delude herself that bureaucrats in Manila would be any more forthright when she interviews them. *Death squads?* she can almost hear them say in the patronizing tone that she's learned to tune out. *You mean like in the backwater barrios down south? Nah, tell your boss there are no human rights violations here. Just your ordinary run-of-the-mill crimes. We've got the peace-and-order situation here under tight control.*

Isabel fantasizes that Elias is sipping cappuccino with her in this café, and she's interviewing him instead. *Is it true there are death squad training camps here, now, in Manila? Were you sent here to run them? Or are you in hiding from them yourself? Do you ever regret joining the DDS? Do you ever regret killing my father?*

And there he is, on the other side of the café's glass wall, gazing at her. "Elias!" she blurts out, and realizes that her voice rings out above the other customers' hushed voices, because they have all stopped to stare. She gestures at him to wait, then hurries outside.

"*Uy*," she says, and gives his arm a light slap. "*Must na, 'dong?*"

"*Maayo man, 'day.*" Elias starts to smile, but the somber expression remains. The shiny scar across his left eyebrow is almost imperceptible. "You're still following me."

Isabel keeps an eye on her laptop through the café's window. "Don't worry, no one will take it."

"You sound so sure."

Elias finally breaks into a smile. "You're safe with me. I'm DDS, remember?"

"Was."

He doesn't respond but asks her instead if she wants a special tour of Intramuros.

"Now? It's after dark."

"The best time of day, if you want to see the *real* Intramuros."

She goes back into the café to retrieve her laptop and deposit it in her room. She decides to leave her bag behind and pocket whatever she needs, so her hands will be free of any encumbrance. A camera, too, would be unwise.

"What? No map?" Elias asks when he sees her empty-handed, making Isabel laugh. "Barrio Santa Lucia has an ancient well at the very heart of it," he says. "Legend has it that nuns threw their aborted fetuses into the well. Would you like to see it?"

Isabel nods.

At the barrio, lightbulbs strung above the narrow alley can be turned on and off by anyone who knows where the switches are. Very convenient for anyone living a fugitive life. "Do you live here?" she asks.

"No," he replies without elaborating further.

She wants to ask if he has a family—and if so, where they are—but she doesn't.

Beneath the Intramuros of contrived nostalgia and simulated refinement is a maze of underground tunnels that neither guidebook, tour guide, nor map hint at. The night guards at every building Elias and Isabel go to are his friends. They all speak Visaya, the language of Davao, and they are very pleased to know that Isabel speaks their language too. They let the two wander around on their own. Elias takes Isabel first to a boys' school that had once been a convent. The guard on duty insists on lending them two flashlights when Elias tells him he wants to show his friend the tunnel. As Elias and Isabel walk through it, they can hear the muffled sound of tricycles mixing with that of horses' hooves and *calesa* wheels grating against the pavement above. They exit the tunnel into the basement of a bank that had once been a monastery. A friendly guard greets Elias there too, calling him "sir."

Isabel wonders aloud if anyone has ever tried a bank heist via the tunnel, and Elias says, "We could do it together. Like Bonnie and Clyde."

Breaking-and-entering was never his thing, Isabel remembers. Elias had gone directly from snatching cell phones to "salvaging" people.

There are three more tunnels underneath former monasteries and convents, and more friendly Visayan security guards in each one. Elias then takes her to the abandoned shell of the largest building of all—a bombed-out cathedral. It is in an out-of-the-way place, obviously a section of Intramuros that the local officials haven't gotten around to making over yet. Promenaders dare not venture there, and not a single tricycle nor *calesa* passes them on the street.

In a corner of the ruins, Elias clears away loose rubble, soil, rocks, and bricks over a square slab of stone before lifting it. A neat, circular hole reveals itself. They go down the stone steps that lead to a cavernous passage. It is two *calesas* wide, two men high, and lined with red adobe bricks. They have gone in only a few steps when Elias points to a pair of skeletons lying prone on a ledge. They are the remains of not very grown people. "Maybe this was the way our Spanish masters got rid of their vermin too," he says.

They walk another five meters to a fork in the passageway. "If we go left, we go out to another former convent. If we go right, we end up at the other cathedral, the one that survived the war. Which one do you want to take?"

Isabel's gaze follows the beam of her flashlight as far as it can go and sees that both tunnels are the same size as the main passage. "The cathedral," she says.

He leads the way. They continue walking until his flashlight shines on the stone steps leading up. She calculates that they'd be underneath the middle of the cathedral now. Here it is absolutely still.

"Turn around, Elias," she says. She has taken a pistol out of her pocket, the only thing she has brought with her on this "tour."

He turns around and the corners of his mouth twitch in amusement. "A mousegun?" he says. Death squad members always use .45-caliber handguns.

"I don't do this for a living."

"No, you don't," he says. Besides, she was never a doer. She always just read and wrote. As he knew her, this was the last thing she'd be able to do. "And you don't want to start. It gets easier after the first." He sees her finger tighten on the trigger. "There are witnesses. All my friends will know it was you."

He means the security guards. But their loyalty is to their job, Isabel knows that much. Not one of them would be likely to come forward to admit that he'd let two trespassers in on his watch.

Elias guesses what she is thinking. "I mean the police. I help them get rid of the vermin here too."

"I have the right credentials. What are yours?"

"You're right. I'm the killer here. You're the defender of human rights."

"Only because I wanted to find you."

"You're blaming me for your father's death? It was you who stole that money. Because it certainly wasn't me. A measly hundred pesos—"

"I tried to make it up to you."

"With sardines?"

"You wouldn't let me give you anything else."

"*Give.* What could you have given?"

He was put in prison with his mother and father even before he'd committed any crime. Anything Elias did after that was bound to be suspect. Isabel understands this. But none of it had been her making. Nor her murdered father's.

Elias makes a grab at the gun.

Back in the café, Isabel resumes writing her letter to the mayor of Manila.

> *Although reports of targeted killings in the Philippines are not new, the number of victims has seen a steady rise over many years. In recent years the geographical scope of such killings has expanded far beyond Davao City on the southern island of Mindanao, to Cebu City in central Philippines, and now to Manila. An already serious problem is becoming much worse.*

There is no end to the vermin needing extermination.

SATAN HAS ALREADY BOUGHT U

BY LOURD DE VEYRA

Project 2, Quezon City

D o you know what *shabu* means? Did you know that each letter means something?" Cesar asked, pressing a clean sheet of aluminum foil between two one-peso coins.

"You mean an acronym," Franco replied, a dull glint of the strip crossing his vision.

"A what?"

"An acronym. That's what you're trying to say. Each letter stands for a word. Like PBA. Philippine Basketball Association. Or NBA . . ."

"I get it. Exactly. An acronym. So . . . you know what shabu means?"

"I didn't know it meant anything."

"Satan Has Already Bought You."

"What?"

"Satan . . . has already bought . . . you," said Cesar, his index finger digging into Franco's shoulder for emphasis. "Satan."

"I don't remember selling anything. Least of all to the devil," said Franco, his gaze still fixed on Cesar's deft hands.

"Satan has already bought you." Cesar tried to sound priestlike.

"So that means he's bought you too, Cesar?"

"I guess. Satan has already bought you. *You too.*"

"Where the hell did you come up with that?" Franco asked.

"Heard it on the radio. Some Christian station."

Franco chuckled. "Wait. Lemme guess . . . that's probably DJ Dan. That holier-than-thou asshole. Did you know he was a major meth-head a couple of years back? You should've heard him when he was still with that station RA 106. Major psycho. Broke up with his wife on air, just before he played some stupid Duran Duran song. Oh, these born-again Christian pricks. Getting high on Jesus is the worst. There's no rehab for that."

"Satan. Has. Already. Bought. You," Cesar muttered under his breath.

"What's with the *You?* Following that logic, it ought to be SHABY. Right? Or it could also mean, Satan Has Already Bought US."

"Just shut the fuck up and gimme that packet already, will you? How much is this worth?"

Cesar's sudden display of impatience shook Franco. "One-five," he replied, giving the small plastic pocket a little shake to loosen the milky crystal bits inside.

Cesar inspected the packet against the light and made a few gentle taps with his index finger. "This definitely does not look like one-five. Are you trying to put one over on me again?"

"Why the fuck would I do that?"

"This isn't the first time, Franco. You know that—"

"Hey, fuck you, man."

"I remember the last time. I just kept my mouth shut. I know you smoked some of my shit at Bing's house."

"That's not true." Franco's protest dissipated into a whine.

"And the one before that. One-five? Looked more like P500 to me. You know you shouldn't be doing that. In other places, you could get killed. You don't fuck around with other people's hard-earned money like that."

"What the fuck are you talking about!"

"Shut up. You're ruining my concentration." Cesar reached

for a pair of scissors, the cheap, plastic kind for grade-schoolers. It was small but its edges were monstrously sharp, ending in frightful angles. *They let kids use these in classrooms?* he thought, then snipped off the top of the plastic packet and placed it once more against the fluorescent light.

"I swear, dude, I didn't smoke from your stash. You gotta trust me."

"Lemme guess. You sent Jong to do the scoring for you, right? You lazy, thieving subcontractor."

"No. Look, you know how these things go. There's no Department of Trade and Industry representative to inspect if they're serving the exact weight. There ain't no customer-complaint desk. One week it's a full packet, the next it's just a fourth. And if you ask why, they'll just say, 'Not enough supply' or, 'Cops shaking us down again,' or some other excuse."

"Yeah, yeah. Just shut the fuck up and hand me that lighter."

Cesar sprinkled a few bits of the meth onto the small aluminum gutter in his hand. Seen from the side, the sheet was folded in an almost perfect V.

The temperature was razor. Cesar felt like his eyeballs were being roasted. They said that Quezon City was the ideal place because it had more trees than, say, Manila or Pasay. Here in Project 2, there seemed to be more greenery per square meter than most cities, but the heat was brutal. It was the kind that broiled brains, which, in turn, lead to stupid decisions, smashed bottles, broken teeth, slashed wrists, and hogtied corpses fished from the river.

Cesar decided to change the subject. "But then there's Precinto Cinco—that's where bad things happen. It's on the corner of Bignay Street and Anonas Road, and it's cursed. No business that has opened beside it has ever lasted, not even a year. Cursed, I tell you."

"What I remember was the Adobo Republic—"

"Not even six months."

"Too bad, cause their adobo was to die for. And before that, there was the pawnshop. I remember the robbery—"

"Two security guards dead. One stabbed in the eye. Cursed!"

"Yeah. Who the hell stabs people in the eye?"

"To be fair, this is good shit." Cesar took another whiff. "Look at how this thing rolls. Beautiful."

Like a distended teardrop, a clear globule slid down the aluminum strip, turning from an opaque yellowish-white into pure white smoke, gently flowing into the small tube tucked between Cesar's lips. The tooter looked like some stylishly alien cigarette.

"Told you. Quality over quantity."

"I still think you cheated me."

"Will you just cut it out, Cesar? Sheesh."

"Good thing you didn't cross a cop. Otherwise, they'd be fishing your body out of the Quirino River by now. Those cops don't have a sense of humor. Especially the ones in Precinto Cinco."

"Those guys are the biggest, nastiest drug dealers in the district," Franco agreed.

"I know. And the last guy who turned out to be a bad customer got his balls cut off. You know where they found his balls? On the counter of Kawilihan Bakery. Imagine buying your early morning *pan de sal* and you see that . . ."

"*Pan de sal* with eggs. Perfect."

"Don't laugh. I think they should do that to you too."

"For the last fucking time, I did not—"

"*Satan has already bought you!*" Cesar yelled, taking Franco by surprise. "Hahaha. Wanna smoke? It's your turn, though I bet you already had your share before coming here."

"My father told me a story," Cesar started a little while later. "They had orders to finish this teenage pickpocket, who was a repeat offender. He was in and out of jail every week, it was almost like he lived there. And the cops got used to the routine, until the kid did something really stupid. He—with his cousin, another worthless druggie—held up a jeepney. It was an improvement over lifting wallets and snatching bags. But, know what? He crossed a line. He cut the finger off this nursing student."

"Why the fuck did he do that?"

"They were in a hurry. Her ring wouldn't come off. So they severed the damn finger."

"Shit."

"Shit, yeah."

"The mom went straight to the police district superintendent. She said she didn't want to press charges. With tears in her eyes, she just gestured with a finger across her throat. There were media people in that meeting. The superintendent was in no position to refuse."

"So what happened to the boy?"

"They killed him, but not without torturing him first. The girl's mom pleaded to the station commander: *Make sure the boy suffers*. Water method."

"You mean they put his head in a drum full of water?"

"No, something worse," Cesar said. "They put the boy's mouth under a faucet. Two cops pull his jaw wide open so it fills up with water. They wait till the boy's belly swells up like a balloon. My dad said he never thought it was possible for a human to suddenly bloat like that in just seconds, like he was pregnant or something. Then they get the biggest, fattest cop to jump up and down on the boy's stomach. I think you know him—Reyes, I think. Big, dark, hairy, and ugly; he drives that battered jeep that passes by here. Water and blood gush out of the boy's ears and nose."

"Ugh. Wait. What happened to the girl?"

"She lived. Although let's just say that when she gets a manicure, she gets 10 percent off."

Franco chuckled.

Cesar took another hit from the aluminum pipe. Thick smoke billowed from his nostrils. "Anyway, that's Precinto Cinco hospitality for you. They're quite a friendly bunch."

"I dunno what's up with that place."

"They found the boy's body by the river," Cesar continued. "You know how the cops get rid of corpses? First they douse the mouth with Tanduay or some gin. That way, it looks like some poor drunk fell into the water and drowned. Brilliant."

"What about gunshot wounds?"

"Oh, they rarely shoot them."

"Bullets too expensive?"

"Well, that . . . but my father says bullets raise more questions. Anyway, when the *barangays* find the bodies, they rarely ask questions. They often know who did it. And it's usually good riddance—it's the same old troublemakers. Same old names and faces, same old tattoos. So you better be careful."

"Just because I have a tattoo—"

"I'm just telling you. Pretty soon the cops are gonna be on your tail. Oh, and you know what the kid was on while he was robbing that jeepney?"

"Lemme guess . . ."

"Satan has already bought you." Cesar took another whiff, the smoke exiting his nostrils.

Franco smiled and repeated the words.

"Human life is so cheap in this town. With all the high gates, the SUVs, you'd think there'd be some sense of order and peace. Middle-class crap. With all this, you'd think we'd be spared from this shit. But no—"

"What do you expect? Your neighbor's the biggest meth dealer in all of Project 2," Franco said.

"You know what Mang Eddie did last year? Meralco found out he was tapping electricity illegally. Of course, the power company first files charges against you. And even if you pay up, they won't turn the lights back on right away. Maybe it's a way of not letting you off so easy. But you know what Mang Eddie did? The man bought a goddamned generator!"

"That is a certified gangster move."

"Certified gangster, my friend. And the generator he got was this cheap secondhand unit. It roared like a bitch across the street all night long, and the whole place stank of diesel. But nobody complained. The barangays wouldn't touch him."

"Not even the cops, I'm sure."

"Well, Mang Eddie used to be a cop. Dismissed from the force."

"Do you buy from him?"

"Nope. Never. The man talks. A lot. If there's one thing I learned, never, ever do business with your neighbor. There's gonna be too many questions. And there's always a problem when a man in this business samples his wares—and, of course, he will. Which means, pretty soon he's gonna get paranoid. *Praning.*"

"Well, that's a risk. But imagine the convenience. He's just, what, less than fifty feet from your house? No more waiting."

"Which only happens when I score from you, Franco. You keep making me wait. Always."

"Will you just—"

"I'm kidding. You're a good boy." Cesar patted his head. Like a dog's.

"You know I don't control these things."

"Uh-huh."

"I go to my source's house, and he'll say someone else is doing the buying. You know that, Cesar. It's a chain of errands. It's endless and, yes, dumb. But what else can I do about it? It's not as if I can buy from the 7-Eleven."

"There's even a rumor that Mang Eddie runs a lab inside his house."

"Big time!"

"Yeah, and I wouldn't be surprised, you know. It's the perfect spot. A large house that looks like shit. Big, angry dogs by the rusty gate. And the smell, Jesus. I don't know whether it's dog shit or some nasty chemical. Some of the other neighbors have complained. But it's not as if the barangay could do anything."

"Man, you've read the news about those meth labs they run in Alabang and Rockwell?"

"Genius, if you ask me. Who would've thought of holing up in those fancy villages? Cause that's the last place the cops would ever think of raiding."

"Those Chinese . . ."

"But it was really the smell that gave them away. Have you ever smelled meth being cooked? It's worse than sulfur, it's worse than shit. The lesson here: so you don't raise a stink, don't let your stuff stink. But this thing, this stuff, Franco," Cesar said after drawing in another whiff, "is really good."

"Told you."

"But I still don't think it's worth one-five."

"I'm never gonna hear the end of this, am I?"

Satan has already bought you. How the fuck did he even think of that? Only a genius meth-head like Cesar could come up with that shit, Franco thought.

"Can I have some more?" Franco gestured to the foil.

"No."

"Why?"

"Cause you already smoked half. More than half, I think."

"Fuck you. I'd never do that to you, Cesar. Come on."

"I've heard stories."

"What stories?"

"And it's not just me you're fucking with."

"Come on!"

"You have a reputation." Smoke curled from Cesar's mouth. He took another hit and kept the vapor in his lungs as long as possible. Two streams of smoke flowed from his nose.

"Damn."

"Human life—so cheap. Especially in these parts," Cesar said. "People today will stab and kill for a bag of peanuts."

"They'd kill for a plate of corned beef," Franco agreed. "Did you see the news?"

"About what?"

"That guy in Tondo. Shot his wife, kids, and in-laws cause the missus wouldn't serve him corned beef while he was drinking. They called it the Pulutan Massacre."

"Oh yeah. See? You don't even need shabu for that shit. All you need is rum. Booze is deadlier than meth, because you can buy it anywhere."

"The things they do in Tondo."

"You don't have to go far. Just last week, on Pajo Street, a kid, nine or ten I think, planted a fork in his sister's eye."

"What is it about this place and eyes getting stabbed?"

"But booze, I tell you. Government keeps blaming drugs for all of society's problems. They should really be looking at the liquor section of these corner stores."

"That's the real nasty stuff. That's how Satan really buys you. Not shabu."

"Nah. Shabu's still something else."

"Yes, it is something else. Booze only fries your brain for a couple of hours, and maybe your liver too. But meth incinerates your brain forever. There's no going back."

"So, Cesar, does this mean our brains are cooked for good?"

"Isn't it obvious? Have you seen a mirror lately? You look like shit."

"You look like shit yourself."

"So we both look like shit. But at least I have a job."

"What is it that you do, really? You never tell me."

"Satan has already bought you," Cesar said.

"No, really."

"What is it I do for a living? I work for Precinto Cinco."

"Hahaha. Good one."

"Your tattoos look stupid."

"What is wrong with you?"

"The last guy they fished from the river had a tattoo on his butt."

"What?"

"It said *Elena,* and there was a broken heart."

"What the fuck are you talking about?"

"They found a broken bottle stuck in his eye, and barbed wire around his neck and hands."

"What?"

"They said it was a drug deal gone wrong."

"What if we go straight to karaoke after we're done?"

"Satan has already bought you."

"Hey . . ."

"That deejay who broke up with his wife on air. Now that's gangster."

"Hey, listen. Let's just relax and get a few drinks. And karaoke," Franco pleaded.

"Where? Pampanguena's? People get stabbed there."

"Well, let's not sing 'My Way.'"

"How can you do karaoke without singing 'My Way'?"

"There are better songs."

"You and your stupid ideas."

"It'll be fun."

"You fucking cheat."

"I wanna sing 'Love Hurts.' I wanna sing Air Supply."

"'Love Hurts' is by Nazareth, stupid."

"Nazareth, Air Supply . . . they're all the same."

"And this definitely ain't one-five. It's you—you fucking cheat. Satan has already bought you." Cesar stood up, went back to his drawer, and pulled out a knife.

"Hey, man, I thought we've been through this—"

Cesar buried the knife in Franco's eye. It was a single blow, swift and sure. Franco staggered, his arms flailing like a man drowning in air that was soaked in smoke, the upper part of his shirt turning a deep crimson.

BROKEN GLASS

BY Sabina Murray

New Manila

Sunday talk and it was all gossip. I sat watching my Tita Baby pick at the *chicharon*, while my mother lit cigarette after cigarette, her smoke rising in an elegant column until the fan—rotating and mounted high on the wall above the dining table—blasted through it. Manong Eddie, our driver, had been sent away the week before and my mother was explaining why.

"You won't believe this," she said. "I was taking my siesta. Eddie wanted an advance on his pay to go the movies, so he parked himself outside my window and started calling, 'Yoo-hoo! Yoo-hoo!' So I called back, 'Who's that yoo-hooing there?' I think he expected me to go downstairs."

"And that's why you fired him?" asked Tita Baby.

"Not just that. Last Sunday, I caught him urinating against the front wall. We were all in the car waiting to go to Mass and I was wondering what was taking so long, so I looked back, and there he was." My mother glanced out to the hallway where my Tita Elena—the eldest of the three sisters—was involved in a lengthy phone call, one that had been going on since my mother and I arrived at her house a half hour earlier. "What's that all about?" asked my mother.

"I'm not sure," said Tita Baby. "But you know Elena's crowd. Those old ladies and their very young, very handsome—"

"—most likely gay yoga instructors," my mother interrupted. "Of course, that's all revealed later, after the money's spent."

"And the champagne has gone flat." Tita Baby pursed her lips, faking sympathy.

From the hallway I heard Tita Elena's voice become animated. She was making her goodbyes now. Tita Baby, my mother, and I all watched as she hung up the phone. Tita Elena had a smile that meant she had a good story to tell. "Sorry, sorry," she said. "Unavoidable."

I wondered what the *tsismis* was.

Tita Elena poured herself a Coke and sat down heavily in a chair. She raised her eyebrows in a meaningful way.

"Elena, both your sisters are here, so who could you possibly be talking to?" asked Tita Baby.

"Ching called."

"Ching?" said my mother. "What did she want?"

"There was a home invasion last night. Or at least an invader." Tita Elena rattled her ice cubes. "Someone tried to break into the neighbor's house."

"Which neighbors?" asked my mother. "Not the Buenaventuras?"

"No, the other side. The de Castros."

"Ay, *Dios mío*," said Tita Baby. "Was anyone hurt?"

"Was anything taken?"

"Actually, no one was hurt, and nothing was stolen," said Tita Elena. "That's what's so strange. Whoever it was disappeared."

"Oh," replied Tita Baby and my mother in chorus.

"It happened like this," started Tita Elena. "Babylon fell asleep on duty, which is no surprise." Babylon was my aunt's security guard. "He's a drunk, you know." I knew well. "He awoke to find himself face-to-face with the invader, a knife pointed straight at his throat." She paused here and looked at me. "Are you sure little Angela should be listening to this? It might give her bad dreams."

"If she can listen to stories of Cherry and her twenty-year-old yoga instructor, she can listen to this," said my mother.

"Well, anyway," Tita Elena continued, "this invader has his knife straight at Babylon's throat and is demanding his gun. Luckily, although Babylon is a *tomador*, he's no idiot. He tells the invader his gun has no bullets. Babylon says that I won't allow him to have a loaded gun because he drinks so much. Remember that night he shot all the chickens?"

"Yes, yes," said Tita Baby impatiently.

"The invader believes him. I mean, if you had any intelligence, you wouldn't be robbing houses, you know."

"You would have a job," said my mother, who has never had a job.

"The second thing Babylon tells him is that the neighbors are far wealthier than we are, which is ridiculous, and that the invader should climb the wall and rob their house instead."

"How on earth can anyone climb that wall?" asked Tita Baby.

"Babylon had to help him."

"That's crazy," said my mother.

"Yes, beyond a doubt, it is," Tita Elena shrugged. "So the invader—at one point standing on Babylon's shoulders—scales the wall and makes it to the top." My tita took a leisurely gulp from her drink. "Once he was at the top, Babylon shot him in the back."

The fan moved slowly from side to side, rustling papers, lifting the bangs off my face. I slapped my leg beneath the table, killing a mosquito. The fan stopped.

"Needs to be fixed," said Tita Elena. "Bebeng," she yelled to the maid, "'*yung bentilador!*"

Bebeng, the head maid, ran out of the kitchen, broom in hand. She hit the fan a few times and it came back to life, grinding a breeze out across the room. The conversation resumed.

"Well, I guess Babylon is worth more than we thought he was," said my mother. "Did you give him the day off?"

My aunt nodded. "I keep thinking that I should call the police, but what's the point? One crook's wearing a uniform, the other crook's dead—"

"But what happened to the burglar?" I asked. "Where is he?"

"You see, that's the mystery," said Tita Elena. "It was so dark that Babylon couldn't make out where the body fell. He was drunk, I'm sure, but he swears he shot him."

"Did you ask the de Castros?" asked my mother.

"Yes, eliminating some of the details of the story. They heard the gunshot, but have no idea what happened to the invader. None whatsoever."

"Very strange," said my mother. "Manila's going to hell. Murders, home invasions, carjackings, all those glue-huffing beggars, and the *sosyal* kids with their—what is it, *shabu*? Yeah, even in our crowd things are getting ugly. Did I tell you why Rocky and her husband are getting separated?" She looked at me thoughtfully. "Angela, go out and play. You're inside all the time. It isn't healthy."

"Do I have to?"

"Yes. Now."

I stood up dutifully and kissed my mother and my titas and crossed the dark wood floorboards, out of the gloom and smoke of the dining room and into the vestibule. The sun outside was shining fiercely, splashing red from the stained-glass doors onto the floor. The invader was bleeding somewhere, or was dead. I heard Tita Baby's voice filtering out of the dining room.

"Rocky's husband couldn't have expected that. It's just not Catholic."

I pushed open the door and stepped onto the front porch. The sun hit my face and every part of my body instantly warmed.

Tita Elena's house had an enormous garden. There was a huge wall around it, like a castle. Someone from Spain had come to put it together right after the war, and once, a long time ago, there had been pet deer wandering around because my Uncle Chuck had liked the look of them. But the deer were gone, along with my uncle, who had died of cancer ten years earlier. Tita Elena was a widow and good at it—still in black and ready for death. The wall was taller than anyone could see over and when we were waiting in the car for Babylon to open the gate, the dirty children would gather around to sneak a look at the lawns and fountains and statues until Babylon shooed them away.

I walked down the tiled steps to the garden. How organized and symmetrical everything looked. Fountain in center, statue in the fountain, a pine tree on the right to match the one on the left, and perfect rows of red and white roses reaching with graceful arms around the lawn. Ligaya was sitting on the bottom step washing clothes. Her muscled arms dipped in and out of the basin, shiny and brown. She was wearing a red bandanna, and her kinky black hair sprung out about her ears. I stepped around to face her. At first, she didn't notice me, she was so intent on her washing, but then she looked up, her lower arms covered in suds.

"Ah, it's you," she said. She smiled at me slyly. Her face was very broad, very dark, and she had the look of a wild animal that had just dropped from a tree. "You've come out to play in the garden."

I nodded solemnly. I was scared of Ligaya.

"Such a pretty dress," she said, grabbing the skirt with a wet hand. "Can I borrow it?"

"I don't think it would fit you," I answered. This sent her into a fit of rich laughter, which echoed across the lawns. The garden seemed strangely deserted.

"Such lovely hair. Almost brown." She reached out and took

my braid in her hand, turning it over thoughtfully. "You could give me some of your hair. It's such beautiful hair."

"My mother said never to give anyone your hair," I responded.

"And why not? Are you scared? Do you think I would put a spell on you? Maybe one day you would wake up and find that I had given you the body and face of an old woman." She smiled, her perfect white teeth standing out against her dark skin. "You know, they shot a man last night. He was on the wall. They shot him and he came tumbling down. He was a bird caught in the tree, but he had no wings to fly away."

I looked up at the wall, to the top, where the broken glass glittered in the sun.

"Listen," said Ligaya, "what do you hear?"

"I hear crickets."

"Crickets and other insects, and birds and the frogs in the fountain," said Ligaya. "And do you know what they're saying?"

I shook my head.

She howled at this, laughing so hard that some of the water sloshed out of the basin. "Maybe they're calling your name, or mine." She squinted to listen better. "No, it's not your name."

"What are they saying?" I asked.

Ligaya listened carefully. "*Have you ever seen a dead man? Have you ever seen a dead man?* That's what they're saying. Can't you hear it?"

I couldn't understand insects, not like Ligaya, who came from the island of Samar, where all witches come from. I looked nervously into the garden.

"Where are you going, Angela? I have a riddle, one that you will like."

"What is it?" I asked.

"He sought a feast and found a bed," she said. "What does

it mean?" I was about to step back but she grabbed my arm. Her eyes lit up. "You'll figure it out, smart thing like you." She let me go. As I ran down the driveway toward the gate, her laughter followed me and I could feel her eyes on my back.

The guardhouse, a small cottage built into the wall by the gate, stood between me and the street beyond. From the other side of the wall, I could hear a junk peddler calling out, "*Dyaryo, bote,*" again and then again. I was out of breath. Ligaya's hand-print, wet on my arm, was disappearing in the heat. Inside the guardhouse, there was snoring, heavy snoring, and the sound of paper rustling gently. I moved to where I could see through the window. Babylon was asleep. There was a half-full bottle of Tan-duay rum beside the chair, next to where his right hand hung down, ready to grasp it when he woke up. His shirt was open and his fat belly hung over his belt. On his lap was a comic book, which was disturbed with every intake of breath. I watched silently. On the floor beside his left hand, I saw the gun.

"Wake up," I said. "Wake up!"

Babylon shook his head and blinked at me.

"Why are you here?" I said. "I thought my aunt gave you the day off."

"Where should I be?" he answered. "This is what I like to do."

"You should be watching a movie. Every time we give our guard a day off, he goes and watches a movie."

"And what kind of movie does he go see? Action? People shooting each other, *boom boom*? I don't need that. Go away. Let me sleep."

"I hear you shot someone."

"Your aunt told you that? Yeah, I shot someone last night."

"Where is he?"

"I don't know."

"Did you kill him?"

"I don't know. Who are you anyway, the police? Maybe I'll shoot you. Go away and let me sleep."

"You're drunk," I said.

"So what? I wouldn't shoot you if I was sober."

We looked at each other as I pondered this and came to believe him. He was better left alone and wasn't going to tell me anything anyway.

I wandered along the side of the house and into the back garden. My aunt kept a huge pig there, beside the maids' quarters. I approached the pen nervously and then stood up on the railing watching it, not minding the smell. The pig was grunting cheerfully, probably hoping that I had brought some treat from the house. It had stiff white hairs on it and little black eyes that seemed to catch everything. I saw Bebeng walk out of the maids' quarters.

"Ah, Angela," she said, "look at this pig, munching away. On your Tita Elena's birthday we will eat him." She looked across the pigpen to the far end of the yard.

"He looks so happy," I said. "Why do we have to kill him?"

"Because that's what we do. Have you ever heard a pig being killed?"

I shook my head.

Bebeng took some rotted greens from a basin by the outside sink and tossed them to the pig. We watched him eat. "Pigs scream. They don't howl like other animals. They cry out, like a man, a man being killed."

I stepped off the railing, suddenly afraid of Bebeng, who had always seemed so kind to me.

"We kill a pig by piercing its neck with a bamboo stick. While he's still alive, we bleed him into a bowl. He screams until he's dead, until we bleed the life out of him. Everything is used. Every last drop of blood has a purpose. Don't feel sorry for that pig. Feel sorry for men, who shed blood so uselessly."

"What men?"

"What?" She hadn't heard me.

"What men bleed?" I asked again.

"What men bleed, what men don't—that's not important. But any blood shed by any man is useless."

Bebeng stood gazing at the pig with a sad smile on her face. She was still there when I walked away.

Past the pigpen, past the maids' quarters, past the shed where the gardeners kept the lawn shears and the buckets for watering the shrubs, was the garage. My aunt kept her three cars there: the Mitsubishi, which she used, the Mercedes that had been Uncle Chuck's and that she couldn't bear to part with but didn't drive, and my cousin's white BMW that had replaced the black BMW after he drove it into a tree. I didn't usually go near the garage. My mother didn't want me hanging around the drivers, but I could hear their laughter. I glanced back at the house. No one was watching, no one that I could see. I tied my shoelace, which had come undone, and went to explore. Manong Cisco, who worked for Tita Elena and lived here, was fiddling with his radio. Manong Pepe, who drove Tita Baby, and Benny, our new driver, were bouncing peso coins off of each other, placing bets, cursing and yelling. Manong Cisco joined in, but he was quiet, and every now and then he would look over at Tita Elena's house as if he thought Benny and Manong Pepe might be too loud. I didn't know why Manong Pepe was always here. Tita Baby only lived one block over and it didn't seem far enough to drive. I watched from behind Tita Baby's Land Rover for a short time before the drivers noticed me.

"Angela!" exclaimed Benny. "Come join with us. You look like you could use some fun."

"I don't know how to play."

"We'll teach you," he said.

"I have nothing to bet."

Manong Pepe laughed hard at this, tearing up, but I did not even smile. Manong Cisco watched me nervously.

"The little señorita has nothing to bet," said Manong Pepe.

"How sad," said Benny. "Do you know what happens to people that have nothing?" He smiled at Manong Pepe, who was patting his bald head with a handkerchief. "Hey, Angela, if you're so smart, answer that. What happens when people have nothing?"

"I don't know."

"Yeah, you wouldn't," said Manong Pepe.

Benny quieted him with a raised hand. "Angela, think hard. People want things that they don't have." He sat back on his heels, squinting against the sun. "You want to play with us, but you have no peso coin. Take his." Benny looked over at Manong Cisco. "Go on. Take your Manong Cisco's. He's not going to say anything."

Manong Pepe laughed again, but I stayed still.

"Yeah, you are smart," said Benny. "I guess you know what happens to people who try to take things around here. Tell her, Cisco. Tell her what happens to them."

"I don't know, *pare*," said Manong Cisco. "What are you talking about? You're gonna scare the kid."

"Not this one," said Benny. He smiled at me as if we shared a secret. "Did you ever want to learn to fly, Angela?"

"Be the shortest flight ever," said Manong Pepe. "You're gonna fly straight down."

Benny laughed loudly with him but then grew quiet. "You know what I'm talking about. I know you do, because you're so smart. I've seen you watching people. And I've been watching you, Señorita Angelita. You hear everything, and you remember, so what do you think happened to that idiot son of a *puta* that tried to break into your tita's house?"

"I don't know," I said. "I asked Babylon. He doesn't know either."

"Shit. Babylon's such a fucking drunk, he doesn't even know what happened to his wife," said Manong Pepe. He slapped Benny's shoulder. When they were through laughing, Benny turned once more to me.

"What do you think, Angela? One second there is a man on the wall, and the next he's gone." Benny studied my face. His eyes were light-colored, like a *mestizo*. I'd heard my mother say Benny thought he was too good to be a driver. "Do you think he flew away?"

I shook my head.

"Here." Benny dug around in his pocket and produced a red rubber ball—the cheap kind from the market. "Why don't you go play with it, Angela, or are you too smart to play?"

"I can play," I responded, holding his gaze. I took the ball and held it. I let it drop on the pavement, catching it after it bounced.

"Now you go play, and when you think you know what happened to that man, the one that flew straight down, you come and tell us, okay?"

I nodded slowly. I didn't like Benny. I was glad to have a reason to leave the garage, to leave the drivers and their game.

At first I just bounced the ball along the pavement, losing it every few times, but this soon lost its charm. I started throwing it in the air a few feet above my head, then higher and higher, until it was just a speck and seemed to hover still in the air before racing downward. I managed to catch it most times. I thought of the invader—the man—the one who flew straight down, like my ball, and threw it higher still, as if this could answer the question. I sent the ball soaring upward until it was nothing but a small red pinprick against a bright blue sky. I threw it again, this time too high. I stood patiently and saw it returning to earth. It was too far away for me to catch. The ball bounced once on the driveway and then again. I chased after it, but it bounced again, ricocheting off a paving stone and landing somewhere in the back garden.

The tangle of the back garden was very different from the front. Trees reached their arms across the small dark paths. The paths wove in and out through the vegetation in ways that I could never remember. The ball had gone to the left, so I headed that way. I looked over my shoulder to see the drivers who stood watching me, now interested. Bebeng too had suddenly appeared and I saw Ligaya with the others, wiping her hands on her skirt. I heard the insects. It was noise I had heard all day, but now the sound was loud. There was the hum of crickets and abruptly the frogs and toads all started to croak. The birds were chirping now, lots of birds, and as I made my way along a path, the sounds grew louder. The broken glass at the top of the wall high above me glittered in the sunlight. The noise was loudest right beside the wall. I was drawn to the sound and to the broken glass shining at the end of the path. And there was the ball, waiting for me. It was in a clump of *makahiya* grass—grass that fainted as my shoes brushed against it. I bent down, the song of the insects humming in my ears, and picked up the ball. There were ants on it, too many ants. In the grass, the ants were moving in an army. I followed them with my eyes and then I saw a huge hand, dark and still, as if it were carved out of wood. A man lay facedown in the long grass, beneath the tangle of vines, in shadow. There were ants, masses of ants marching over my feet, crawling off the ball and down my arms, marching to that rising hum of noise and life in the garden. The ants were moving onto the body in two straight columns. There was a hole in his back, a hole from which he had bled, soaking his shirt, leaving wet sticky clumps on the grass. The noise of the garden was too loud now and made me wonder whether it was really insects and frogs, or rather a strange echo in my head. I smelled the blood above the fragrant frangipani, above the rotting leaves. The man's head was turned to one side as if he were sleeping and I crouched down to see his face, the eyes shut tight with thick lashes, his mouth slightly open with still, full lips—he was somehow held in a dream, in a better sleep than the cold dead that happened with guns and invasions and guards and walls. He had the sleep of a tired man who could never be woken up, who would go on dreaming forever.

AFTER MIDNIGHT

BY Angelo R. Lacuesta

J.P. Rizal

When we finally roll out, our seats are pitched up like we're on a plane lifting from the tarmac. My window's open a crack and I'm breathing the firecracker fog like I'm swimming in it.

A harness of greasy chains moors us to the truck. There's a little bit too much give. We lag a couple of seconds on the turns and sway loosely whenever there's enough room to accelerate. The truck hits a pothole and we feel it late because our front wheels are off the ground.

There are still people out at this hour. They're gawking at us as we rumble down the street. They look like they've never seen a smashed car and a tow truck in their lives. The girls are on the sidewalks sitting in plastic chairs with their butts out and their elbows on their knees. The glow of big-screen TVs is pumped out from the shadows in the doorways behind them. They look at me like I'm the one to feel sorry for and I can almost hear them clucking to themselves.

It doesn't matter. It's way after midnight now, and I'm far from the places where there are people I know. Actually, we really aren't that far, but there's a big difference between that side and this side and J.P. Rizal is the line in the middle.

The driver's arm darts out of the truck window to flick a cigarette into the haze. I try my best to remember their faces but it's too dark. I should have told them which route to take home but it's pretty straightforward and I feel like they're doing me a favor and I don't want to mess things up. It's New Year's Eve and nobody would take my business and these guys came all the way from Caloocan or something like that.

I switch on the stereo even though I'm fully expecting it not to work. Instinct, I guess. While I'm still trying to remember what we were listening to before it happened, the speakers blast Patsy Cline singing "Walkin' After Midnight." Everything starts coming together.

She was messing with her phone, trying to make calls, trying to text, cursing every time it failed. A security guard came over waving his big flashlight in the air. He asked us if we were okay and I asked him if he knew the number of a towing company. He said no and walked over to my car shaking his head like it was his property or like this was any of his business. People get drunk, people get crazy this time of the year, the security guard was saying. I was in the middle of making all these calls and I got in his face and he sort of backed off. He was thinking maybe I was the one who was drunk or crazy on something. I gave him attitude, like things could be worse, buddy—it could be you instead of me. I stood around like I was a congressman and the pale girl with me was some hot starlet, when all I am is a guy making a living writing ad copy.

We heard the truck coming before we saw it. I was just about to give up and leave the car right in the middle of the street. The front of it was a lopsided mess but the rest of it was still an unmarred black, the nighttime sheen on the hood cutting through all that gunpowder smoke in the air.

There was a thin man and a fat man. It would have been funny if they weren't there to tow my car. The fat man was just the driver and the muscle. He unloaded the chains from the truck and went under the car to hook them up. The thin man did most of the talking. He told us there was no room in the truck and we needed to get back into the car. I'd never been in any situation like this so it seemed like the most logical thing to do. I'd considered hailing a cab and making a convoy but it was all too much trouble.

We crawled back inside and the fat man pulled on another chain coming off the pulley. The tires lifted from the ground and the car jerked on the chains like it was a little toy. He kept pulling until I heard the front grill crunch hard against the top of the pulley. I gripped the steering wheel like an idiot and Andy giggled. She looked like every bit of her was ready to party again. She had her legs folded under her thighs and she was smoking a cigarette, just like I'd found her earlier, sitting and smoking in the VIP section at Club Vetica as if she'd been born there, which as far as I know is the only way you ever get into the VIP section of any joint worth going to.

She had someone else's hand on her knee and it belonged to Gil Gordon. I recognized the congressman from the south because he was in the papers that morning. She was in the middle of shouting something to somebody but I didn't want to waste a second. I waved to her across the velvet rope and I wasn't surprised that it took a while for her to recognize me. She stood and bent across the barrier to kiss my cheek and I smelled the booze on her breath. The congressman kept staring, wondering who the fuck I was.

They were playing hip-hop and it was really music for the cheapskate New Year's Eve crowd, but we danced anyway. People hardly dance in clubs anymore. Everyone just stares at everyone else, worried that everyone else is having a better time. Gil Gordon was now staring at my hand on the small of her back, and it felt wet with sweat. I thought of what chances I'd have against him. I couldn't even remember the last time I'd made a fist.

Andy's mouth was moving but I couldn't hear what she said. I moved my face close to hers and put my ear right next to her mouth. She was asking me if I wanted to do a couple of lines. I never say no to that, so I tailed her into the bathroom, where they pumped the music in so it was like a little club built for two. When we came out, Gil Gordon was blocking the doorway with a funny smile on his face.

My father once told me that in a fight, I should never look into the other guy's eyes. He told me to focus on the little spot where the eyebrows meet. As soon as I clocked Gil Gordon right on the jaw I thought it was probably the first successful punch I'd ever thrown. Blame it on the music. Blame my next punch on the way Andy was looking at me. I would have thrown another if the bouncers hadn't stepped in. The way they handled the situation you could tell it happened a lot, except that maybe this was kindergarten stuff compared to the things that sometimes went down.

I can't remember if Andy grabbed my hand or it was the other way around, but the next thing I knew we were getting into my car. Drive fast! she yelled. Don't think, let's go! One-two-three. That's how my father taught me things happen in commercials.

Andy was all giddy. She had her bare feet up on the dashboard and kept playing with her phone. She said she wanted to text her friends about what went down at the club, but she just couldn't type properly. Fucking autocorrect! I said she didn't need to, her friends were bound to find out soon enough. The way shit like this spreads. Manila is so small, I said. It's twenty million people but I was talking about the people and the places we knew. Shit, she said, shit. You shouldn't have done *that*. She couldn't help but laugh again, briefly caressing my cheek with her hand. Not that guy. You shouldn't have done that.

I drove hard until we had gone past the Makati skyline and we were on my side of town, whizzing past the dark apartment buildings and the shophouses on J.P. Rizal. I swung a hard left and we were on my street. You can't miss the building where I live because there's an InstaPure water refilling station on the ground floor and a twenty-four-hour Mini-Stop right across from it. There's an elevator but it takes forever and we were still really lit so we walked up ten flights to my floor. I didn't know what she'd think of my shit apartment but I mostly didn't care.

I took a couple of joints out of a jar in the fridge. We smoked them and we didn't really move, not for what seemed like hours, and it felt unnatural when we lifted our hands to smoke or shifted our legs. The only thing that felt easy was talking.

She asked me what I did for a living, who my parents were, what they did. Things you never really ask when you're in a club. I told her I was an adman, just like my father had been. Remember that TV spot where a girl walks into a bar full of men and orders the nonalcoholic beer? That snap election commercial where the female candidate confesses that she's just a woman and isn't really fit to run the country? All my father's. But talking about it that way somehow made it mine, as if I could inherit things like that instead of money.

When I grew tired of talking Andy asked me to take her home. We were both exhausted, though the weed had done much to make us forget what had happened earlier. It was still dark outside. It was maybe four in the morning when we stepped out of the apartment into the thick smoke of last night's firecrackers, holding our breath until we got back into my car.

There were clusters of people out on the streets drinking gin and beer and lighting up whatever firecrackers were left. I thought I could hear each bang go off separately. We saw a couple of punks at the intersection ahead lighting up some stuff, waiting to toss it under the car as we drove past.

The shape appeared in front of us like it was formed out of

fog, an SUV in a straight path toward us. I saw Gil Gordon at the wheel, his face briefly lit by the splash of headlights across his windshield. His elbow rose at the last second to shield his face and swerve at the same time. He fishtailed and his rear flank spun toward us.

I thought about my mother who never had to work a day in her life, until my father died from of all sorts of complications following a stroke. It followed a long night of work, following a successful pitch, following a long-wished-for promotion. Which is why I drove his car—the only thing he had passed on to me—for fourteen years before I earned the company car plan. I drove my mother around—to the grocery, to the mall where she watched one movie a week, to my aunt's office in Legaspi Village where she did part-time work. And my mother kept reminding me to drive carefully, reaching over to knock on the speedometer loudly whenever I went over whatever speed limit she had in mind at the time, because she was sitting in what she called the "death seat." The kind of catchy phrase my father would have invented to scare enough shit out of people to make them want to buy whatever he was selling—hand cream because chores caused sores, mouthwash because gingivitis would eat up your gums, disinfectant soap because things had consequences and your conscience would never forgive you.

I asked Andy if she was okay and she said yes she was. I brushed my hands over her body from her scalp to her ankles. I wasn't sure what I was looking for—broken bones, maybe, or the sudden wetness of blood, but I didn't find anything. I kept asking if she was okay and she waved me off and was already trying to make a call on her smashed phone.

My cell phone's gone dead. The fat man sticks his arm out again, a fresh cigarette between his fingers, a tattoo of someone's initials on his forearm. For a moment I think I see the driver flicking a firecracker in my direction. I bang my fist on the horn and get nothing but the sound of plastic being punched.

An explosion makes my ears ring and I can hear the blood throbbing like it's trying to find a way out of my head. I can't hear the music anymore. The smoke fills the car and it's making me sleepy, but something tells me we're back on J.P. Rizal again. Andy's leaning back against the headrest. Her face is frozen and her mouth is in the shape of an O, looking like it's right in the middle of singing a song.

PART II

Black Pearl of the Orient

Quezon Ave.

GMA Kamuning

Cubao

Santolan

Ortigas

†RESE

THIRTEEN
STATIONS

Guadalupe

Buendia

Ayala

Magallanes

Budjette Tan   KaJo Baldisimo

1:03 AM

CAPT. GUERRERO OF THE PHILIPPINE NATIONAL POLICE IS NORMALLY UNPERTURBED BY REPORTS OF GHOST SIGHTINGS IN MRT STATIONS.

BUT IN THE PAST WEEK, THE REPORTS HAVE STARTED TO COME IN MORE FREQUENTLY.

Ortigas

AND WHEN THINGS TAKE A TURN FOR THE WEIRD, OR IN THIS CASE, WEIRDER THAN USUAL, THAT'S WHEN HE CALLS ALEXANDRA TRESE.

GOOD MORNING, ALEXANDRA. I GOT A REPORT FROM THE BOYS DOWN IN ERMITA. THEY SAW YOU RUNNING AFTER A TEEN-AGE GIRL.

SHE WAS AN ASWANG, PRETENDED TO BE A CALL GIRL. SLAUGHTERED THREE CUSTOMERS IN ONE OF THE CLUBS. WE TRACKED HER AND TOOK HER DOWN. SO, YES, I GUESS YOU CAN SAY IT'S A GOOD MORNING.

SO, WHAT'S BEEN KEEPING YOU AWAKE, CAPTAIN?

THESE DAYS, THE DEAD HAVE BEEN KEEPING ME AWAKE.

"EARLY THIS WEEK, WE GOT A REPORT FROM THE QUEZON CITY STATION. THREE NAKED FEMALES, SEEN INSIDE THE MIDDLE CAR. AN EYEWITNESS SAID THEY WERE ALL BLOODY AND BRUISED, THEN THE LIGHTS FLICKERED AND THE YOUNG WOMEN VANISHED."

"AT FARMER'S MARKET STATION, A MAN WITH HALF A HEAD WAS SEEN STUMBLING OUT OF THE TRAIN. THE SECURITY GUARD RAN TO CALL FOR HELP, BUT WHEN HE CAME BACK THE MAN WITH HALF A HEAD WAS GONE."

"HALF A HEAD, HOW ORIGINAL."

THIS IS THE SPOT WHERE CHARLIE AND MICHAEL MARTINEZ DIED. FATHER AND SON. THEY EXHIBITED ALL THE SIGNS OF SOMEONE WHO WAS TRAPPED IN A FIRE AND DIED OF SMOKE INHALATION.

CCTV SHOWED NO SIGNS OF A FIRE EVER HAPPENING IN THE TRAIN. THE VIDEO DID SHOW THEM RUNNING, TRYING TO ESCAPE, CLAWING AT THE DOOR. THEY STARTED SCREAMING AND GASPING FOR AIR. FINALLY, THEY JUST COLLAPSED.

CAPTAIN, CAN YOU HAVE THE CONDUCTOR TAKE US TO BUENDIA STATION?

SURE. NOT A PROBLEM. BUT WHY?

BECAUSE, BASED ON ALL THE REPORTS, BUENDIA IS THE ONLY STATION WHERE NO GHOSTS HAVE BEEN SEEN. WHY ISN'T IT HAUNTED? EVERYTHING JUST SEEMS TO END THERE.

FOR NOW, CAN I HAVE THE CAR TO MYSELF?

I COULD SENSE THAT THE SPIRITS BOARDED AT GUADALUPE STATION. THAT'S WHERE THE EMBERS END.

THANK YOU, GREAT SANTELMO.

MAY THE GREAT LIGHT SHINE UPON YOU.

CAPT. GUERRERO, WASN'T THERE A BIG FIRE IN THE GUADALUPE AREA YESTERDAY? THE SMOKE WAS SEEN ALL THE WAY IN MANILA.

Buendia

YES, IT WAS A SQUATTER'S AREA. CASUALTIES ALMOST REACHED A HUNDRED. AS USUAL, THE FIRE TRUCKS COULDN'T GET IN TO HELP BECAUSE OF THE NARROW STREETS.

WAIT! YOU'RE ALIVE? YOU'RE NOT EVEN ALLOWED TO BE ON THE TRAIN!

I AM ALEXANDRA TRESE! WHO ARE YOU? AND WHO TOLD YOU THAT YOU COULD USE THESE TRAIN TRACKS?

OH! A TRESE! SO SORRY, MA'AM! I DIDN'T KNOW.

I AM A TAGA-SUNDO FROM IBU. I'M JUST THE DELIVERY GUY. DON'T KILL ME.

IBU? SINCE WHEN DOES THE GODDESS OF DEATH USE THE MRT TO FERRY THE SOULS OF THE DEAD?

THE TRAIN TRACKS FOLLOW THE PATH OF IBU'S RIVER, WHICH LEADS TO THE AFTERWORLD. JUST THOUGHT IT WAS THE MORE EFFICIENT WAY TO GO. WE THOUGHT NO ONE WOULD MIND OR NOTICE IF WE DID IT LATE AT NIGHT.

EXCEPT WHEN NEARLY A HUNDRED GHOSTS SUDDENLY SURGED INTO THE TRAIN AND CAUSED THE DEATH OF THAT FATHER AND SON.

I...WELL... WE DIDN'T EXPECT THAT.

THE ONLY REASON I AM ALLOWING YOU TO CONTINUE THIS OPERATION IS BECAUSE THESE PATHWAYS ORIGINALLY BELONGED TO IBU.

BUT FROM NOW ON, YOU CAN ONLY BRING IN YOUR PASSENGERS AFTER THE MRT HAS STOPPED OPERATIONS, AFTER MIDNIGHT. YOU UNDERSTAND THESE CONDITIONS?

YES, MA'AM. THANK YOU, MA'AM.

THREE DAYS LATER

I'M SORRY, WE'RE STILL CLOSED.

I'M HERE TO SEE ALEXANDRA TRESE. I HAVE BEEN SENT BY THE LADY IBU.

IT'S OKAY, HANK. LET THEM THROUGH.

DID IBU SEND YOU TO CONTEST THE CONDITIONS I SET FOR THE USE OF THE RAILWAYS?

NO, MA'AM. SHE SAID SHE WOULD LIKE TO MAKE AMENDS FOR NOT ASKING PERMISSION IN THE FIRST PLACE.

A GODDESS OF DEATH RARELY NEEDS TO MAKE AMENDS WITH ANYONE.

THE LADY IBU SAID THAT WHEN THE SIXTH CHILD OF THE SIXTH CHILD CHOOSES HER PATH, SHE WOULD LIKE TO BE IN YOUR GOOD GRACES.

THEIR SOULS CAME ABOARD AT QUEZON BOULEVARD STATION.

WE'LL TAKE YOU THERE. FROM THE STATION, FOLLOW THE MARIPOSA. THESE WHITE MOTHS ARE LADY IBU'S SOUL SEEKERS.

SINCE THAT TIME, THEY HAVE BEEN THE EVER-LOYAL PROTECTORS OF TRESE.

WHEN ASWANG GO TO SLEEP THEIR NIGHTMARES ARE FILLED WITH THE BONE-WHITE MASKS OF THE KAMBAL AND THE SILVER BLADE OF TRESE'S KRIS.

BUT NOW, THEY ARE LEGION AND FEEL NO FEAR AS THEY ATTACK.

FOOLISH, HUNGRY ASWANG.

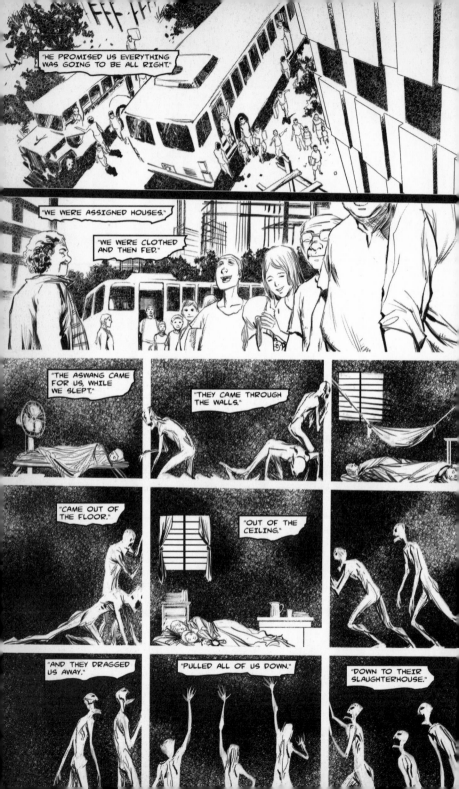

I'LL HAVE MY MEN START LOOKING FOR DE LA STRADA.

ACTUALLY, CAPTAIN, THE MORE IMPORTANT QUESTION IS, WHERE CAN I FIND THE MAYOR NOW?

"ON A NIGHT LIKE THIS, HE'S USUALLY AT THE DOMINION."

DOMINION

STOP RIGHT THERE! GO BACK TO THE END OF THE LINE!

"THE DOMINION CLUB THE ONE OWNED BY DOMINIC VILLACERAN. SELF-PROCLAIMED PRINCE OF ASWANG."

MR. MAYOR, WHERE IS MR. DE LA STRADA? SEEMS LIKE NO ONE KNOWS WHERE HE IS THESE DAYS.

GOOD EVENING TO YOU TOO, MS. TRESE.

COMFORTER OF THE AFFLICTED

BY F.H. BATACAN

Lagro

The neck is broken. That's why the head is turned at such an unnatural angle. The body is lying chest down on the floor, but the head tilts upward and twists sharply to the right, a rotation of more than ninety degrees. The eyes are open, staring. Something in that frozen expression makes Saenz think she did not go down meekly. Her fingernails are rimmed with gunk from where she scratched her attacker, raked flesh, drew blood.

Senior Inspector Mike Rueda stands quietly behind the priest, waiting.

Saenz straightens up from a crouching position over the body with a slight groan.

"You okay, Father?" Rueda asks.

"I'm an old man," Saenz mumbles, almost to himself. He strips off the latex gloves, presses the heel of his left hand against his right eye to relieve the pressure there. He is about to absentmindedly stuff the bloodstained gloves into the pocket of his jeans when Rueda reaches out to stop him.

For a man with a prizefighter's face, Rueda is surprisingly gentle. "Let me take those." He holds open his own gloved hand. Saenz realizes his mistake, grunts, and hands the gloves over. He glances down at his jeans and notices a small red streak where the gloves have made contact with the denim.

"Like I said, Mike. An old man."

Rueda bags the gloves. "You need a vacation." He shrugs at the woman's body. "Well, maybe after this one." He turns, motions for a young officer to take the small bag for disposal. When she's out of earshot, he moves closer to the priest. "So was it the broken neck, or the glass?"

She had fallen from the stairs onto a glass-top table. The blood pooled beneath her head was from where a large sliver of glass had lodged itself in her brain.

"Either, both," Saenz shrugs. "What matters is, was she pushed?" He glances up at the stairs, waving long fingers toward a section of the balustrade near the top that had given way. "You try a fracture-match on that, and I'm guessing the stress marks will be consistent with a forceful impact. Not with any mere weakness in either the structure or the material." Back to the woman now, fully absorbed in her face. "Gave him hell, though. Her luck ran out at the top of the stairs, but before she went down, she made him suffer nearly as much as she did."

Rueda surveys their surroundings. Books have fallen off shelves, picture frames knocked off walls, furniture overturned. "Satisfied it's a *him*, then?"

Saenz nods. "There's a full-length mirror on the door of one of the bedrooms. It's cracked. Nothing lying around it, and a bit of blood and hair at the point of impact. So what cracked it was a someone, not a something. Someone's head, in fact."

"And it's a *him* because . . . ?"

"The hair is short." A note of exasperation lends a slight edge to Saenz's voice. "And the point of impact is a few inches above where it would have been, had that head been hers. She's, what—about 5'5", 5'6"? Bit taller than the average woman here. So if the person who cracked the mirror is even taller, odds are it's a man."

Rueda takes a deep breath, biting down his own frustration.

Father Augusto Saenz is a forensic anthropologist by training, and technically his expertise wouldn't be needed for cases like this. But if Rueda and his people could see things as clearly, connect the dots as quickly as the Jesuit does, he wouldn't be asking him to his crime scenes so often. "Okay. I'll make sure someone gets samples from the mirror too."

Saenz doesn't answer, doesn't even seem to have heard. He is still looking intently into her face. "You brave girl," he mutters. "You brave, brave girl."

Her parents have been arguing for what seems like hours, but suddenly the shouting stops.

They told her to stay downstairs but she needs to know if it's all right to come up now, if they're going to start making dinner soon. So she creeps up the stairs and then she hears it, *thud-thud-thud*, like someone hitting the wall with a fist, then gasping, panting, whispered words that she can't quite understand.

When she opens the door, her father has his hand around her mother's throat, and he is pounding her face against the headboard.

Blind instinct, blind rage, blind something else that the child can't understand makes her rush toward them, makes her clamber up the bed and onto his back. She grabs great thick fistfuls of his hair, tugs hard, and he releases his grip on her mother, pulls himself up from where he has been looming over the woman and pinning her down. He turns his attention to the screaming six-year-old on his back, and with one easy motion flings her off.

The child falls and hits her head on the floor, pain blooming a dozen colors in her field of vision before bleeding into white, but she gets up and lunges for him, all fingernails and elbows and tiny sharp teeth. And he knocks her back just as easily as the first time, and still she comes back for more.

The fourth time she comes at him, he picks her up by an arm, shoves her out of the room, and locks the door. The child doesn't know it yet, but her shoulder has been dislocated.

Under ordinary circumstances, someone would have heard. The Lagro house is in a subdivision carved out of the side of a hill, and although each house is built on its own little plot of land and surrounded by concrete walls, someone would still have heard something. The living room had been a wreck when Saenz, Rueda, and his team arrived; the bedrooms only slightly less so. When she fell from the stairs, it was likely that she screamed. When her body landed below, the glass table had shattered on impact. Either of the two would have woken someone.

But everyone was awake, and still nobody heard anything. A much bigger racket was drowning it all out. It was New Year's Eve when the killer came into her home, and nobody heard them battling it out above the din of firecrackers, blaring car horns, paper trumpets, random gunfire, and people shouting and singing in the streets. He could not have chosen a better time to strike.

Saenz is sure of one thing: she knew the man. She knew him, and she had let him in. She was polite. She made coffee. She served cookies. They talked, they drank. Somewhere between coffee and her neck breaking, something happened, an argument perhaps. He had flung her around the room, but she had flung him right back. She had been a strong woman, and she didn't make it easy for him. If a neighbor hadn't made an excess of potato salad for *medianoche*, brought it over to share with Libby, taken the open gate as an invitation and the ajar front door as a warning, Libby's body might not have been found for days.

Saenz had taken a picture of her before they removed her body. His phone is filled with dead faces. He remembers each and every one of them, the ones he could help and the ones he couldn't. The faces are mostly slack and blank. Sometimes the fear is unmistakable, drawn plain in the wide eyes, the twist of the open mouth.

Her dead face is different, neither blank nor afraid. When he goes to bed he tries to forget it, but her face stays in his mind, hovering in the darkness there. Several times in the night he is compelled to look at the photograph. *Just one more time, this will be the last, I've got to get some sleep.*

He finally recognizes what's written on her face: not fear, but fury.

She's fourteen. She comes home from school one day, her mother is sitting on the kitchen floor. There is broken glass everywhere, shards of plates whose patterns she can still recognize.

She knows her mother will be sitting on the floor like this for a while. She takes a broom and a dustpan and begins to sweep carefully around the woman.

When they go shopping for new plates days later, the girl suggests to her mother, with deliberate nonchalance, that they buy plastic ones. "It's cheaper," she explains, and leaves it at that.

Her name was Olivia Delgado—Libby. She was thirty-nine, and she lived alone. She read a lot, and liked Jack 'n' Jill potato chips (twelve packs in three different varieties in the kitchen cupboard). Libby didn't seem to have many friends, if her profile page on one of those social networking websites is anything to go by. She wasn't pretty, but in her pictures she looked straight into the camera, relaxed, confident, the barest hint of a smile at the corners of her mouth. She wasn't into sports but had climbed six mountains, wasn't much into clothes but had forty-three pairs of shoes.

Saenz wants to pull aside and question the few people at her memorial service—relatives, friends, colleagues. But they recognize him from the television news; they know who he is and what he does for the police, and they actually go out of their way to avoid him. He finds this odd. He tells Rueda a few days later and Rueda grimaces.

"I thought you priests were trained to be sensitive. You didn't think it was a bad time to be asking questions?"

"I was trying to help," Saenz snaps.

"I know, Father. I didn't mean to—"

Saenz waves him away. "No, you're right. It was . . . inappropriate."

Rueda has known Saenz for decades. When the priest was younger, he used to be genial, easygoing. Over the years, however, he has grown quieter, more guarded. He still looks preternaturally young—Saenz in his sixties remains a showstopper of a man—but his eyes are ancient, haunted. He's prone to irritability and ill temper. It's difficult now for Rueda's younger officers to believe that the priest who comes to their crime scenes every once in a while ever used to be a "nice man." At best he's reserved; at worst he's testy and dismissive. And he's always in a rush, always telling people to hurry up. Age slows most people down, but then again Saenz isn't most people. If anything, age seems to have sped him up, downright turbocharged him, with little patience or understanding to spare for anyone who can't keep up.

Rueda thinks Saenz is racing to finish as much as he can, while he still can.

He slides a notepad across the table to the older man. There's a list scribbled on the top page. "I don't have enough people to do this, and I've got my hands full till Wednesday."

Saenz rips the page off and folds it neatly, slips it into his shirt pocket, makes for the door. Rueda is grateful but he doesn't say anything. They know each other well enough that such niceties are no longer necessary.

* * *

She's sixteen, old beyond her years, and finally escapes high school. It's time for her real life to start, she's good at math, she chooses a major. She keeps everyone at bay because people are always asking questions she doesn't want to answer.

She's seventeen, she tries out for the swim team and makes the dean's list, her mother breaks and heals and breaks again. She's eighteen, she passes her driving test. She wants to wait for her father outside his office and run him down, back up, and drive over him, again and again in a loop until there's nothing left but a stain on the concrete. It's a fantasy, she knows she can't do it, so she studies hard, she applies herself. She sees the future as a dark tunnel through which she must pass to get to the light, dragging her mother behind her.

She graduates with honors, gets three offers almost instantly, and chooses the best, not the one that pays the most. She combs through real estate listings, claws her way to independence. She learns to climb mountains. She bides her time.

The people on the list are cooperative. Which is a bit of a waste since they seem to know very little about Libby Delgado. Worked at a foreign bank, in a fairly senior position. Comfortable but not rich. Parents dead. No siblings. Bought the Lagro house a little over a decade before. Rented an apartment closer to her work-place but always spent the weekends in Lagro. Didn't employ a maid or any kind of household help. Kept to herself. The people on the list are perfectly helpful but also perfectly opaque.

Something itches in Saenz's brain, sly and relentless and maddeningly out of reach.

He asks to be let into her house again. Rueda comes with him. Everything remains as they had left it on New Year's morn-ing. She had few relatives, and she wasn't very close to any of them. There has been no mad scramble for her worldly possessions, something rare in this part of the world.

Saenz walks through the house, muttering to himself. Rueda follows him around, careful not to distract him. The priest stops at a small utility room just off the kitchen, looks down at a little pile of clothing dumped on the floor beside the washing machine. *Odd.* Then he walks a little farther down and finds a tiny bathroom.

"Your boys dust in here?" he asks.

"Guest bathroom? Yes."

Saenz fully alert now, almost buzzing. "The coffee cups."

A beat, then Rueda understands. "You think he used the bathroom. You want to see if we can find a match."

"The living room was trashed, and the upstairs. But no other signs of struggle or disarray anywhere else." The priest moves back toward the washing machine, his eyes narrowing to focus on the pile of clothes on the floor. "Except in here."

He bends to pick up a blouse, and the rest of the small pile comes up along with it. He is momentarily confused and then he realizes that they're all still attached to a small, blue plastic clothes rack. Saenz carefully plucks through the clothing until he finds what he is looking for.

"Hook's broken."

Rueda comes closer. "So it was torn off the—"

Saenz darts off before he can even finish, looking around for a pole or makeshift clothesline—anywhere the rack could have been hung from. He finds the broken-off plastic hook on the floor of the shower stall in the guest bathroom.

"It was hanging from the shower curtain pole," Rueda says, trying desperately to follow the priest's mental leaps. "You think he saw it when he used the bathroom. It set him off." He turns to Saenz. "But why?"

Saenz unclips the flimsy little blouse from the rack, holds

it up by the shoulder seams. He tosses it on top of the washing machine, takes another tiny article of clothing from the rack. Pink T-shirt, held up, examined, tossed. Nude brassiere. Matching panties.

Finally, he looks at Rueda, those strange light-colored eyes burning. He grabs the clothes with one hand, thrusts them almost in the police officer's face. "Libby Delgado was not a small woman."

She puts a down payment on the house on Caridad Street because the neighborhood is quiet and there is greenery all around it; it's not far from La Mesa watershed, the air is cleaner than elsewhere in the city. When she looks up at the night sky, she can see hundreds of stars.

She puts a down payment on the house because it is isolated and not easy to find. The house has high walls and a sturdy gate. It's in a part of the city that is still considered too far from the center of things. The area is underdeveloped; there aren't many public transport options. People imagine that rapists and the ghosts of the unquiet dead lie in wait in the *carabao* grass grown tall and wild in the vacant lots that line its highways and streets. They're not too far wrong—a bloated body is dumped in the grass nearly every other month. It isn't until years later that the megamalls set up shop, and developers start snapping up the land and property values shoot up. Most of the grass is cleared away but the ghosts linger.

She puts a down payment on the house and never tells anyone where it is, so that it will be easier to keep her mother safe. She's not so afraid of ghosts, but she knows that monsters are real.

"We're assuming someone else was staying with her. Another woman." Rueda hands the priest a mug of coffee, black and strong, just the way he likes it. "Who was she? Was she there when Libby was killed?"

Saenz shakes his head. "It's not a big house. If someone else was there, she would have been found, she would have been dragged into that massive struggle somehow. You only have two blood samples, Libby's and the killer's. Highly unlikely that whoever owned those clothes was there when Libby died."

"Who, then? Houseguest? Lover?"

"Don't know." Saenz scowls into the liquid in his mug. "Don't know who Libby Delgado is, either."

"Sure we do, we—"

"No," the priest cuts him off sharply. "Don't fall into that trap, Mike. We know only what she wants us to know. We need to find out what she's hiding."

Saenz talks like she's still alive.

The house can't hold her mother; she eventually goes back to her husband, thinks that he can be saved, that this is what a good, strong Catholic marriage should be. It's funny-sad, when Libby thinks about it. She lost her own faith ages ago. God is dense, deaf, dead, a one-trick pony, putting people on this earth only to forget about them.

The next time God forgets about them, she calls the police. Later, she calmly gives testimony. Her father is put away for a while, but he gets out soon after, slap on the wrist, that's just how it is. Her mother stays and stays. Libby tells her, *You can always come live with me. But you have to choose.* She almost says, *You have to choose me.* But she doesn't, because it won't happen. And she cannot keep dashing herself over and over again on the jagged, treacherous rocks of her parents' lives.

She never speaks to them again. Cancer kills her mother before her father can, a minor miracle. She goes to the funeral but she stands way off in the background, where nobody can see her. When she gets home, she throws every photograph, every keepsake, every card and gift and letter—every single thing that reminds her of her family—into a box. Then she marches out into the backyard and sets the box on fire. She stands close, sticks a hand briefly into the licking flames to see how it feels: the bonfire of her history.

Watches it all burn.

Libby's desktop and laptop computers are filled with spreadsheets, charts, graphs, and documents for work. When she surfed the Internet, she checked the market indices, read newspapers, shopped for books and shoes. Her bookmarks include dozens of news websites, online booksellers, auction sites. She did not maintain a blog, did not keep a diary of her thoughts, at least not one that Saenz has discovered. And although he can easily ask Rueda to find someone who could sniff out her electronic trail, hack into her e-mails, an acute sense of propriety prevents him from doing so. Her planner does not give him much to work with, either. Aside from meetings at work, she recorded little of her life, a few lunches and dinners, the occasional party.

But after thumbing through it for the fourth time, the priest notices something. There are appointments with people whose names she spells out clearly—*Vicki* and *Faye* and *Jorge*—and others where she only writes initials. It could be something, it could be nothing, but it's unusual. People often write a certain way and stick with it—names, dates, numbers. It becomes second nature, instinctive. To write full names for some and initials for others, it's a deliberate thing. *Why would you do that? Why don't you want us to know who you were meeting? AS and FJ and the last one, first appearing in late October, EV? Who were they?*

Her latest credit card statement arrives a few weeks after her death. Rueda forwards it to his office along with the rest of the mail, just bills and flyers. Saenz studies the document carefully.

You bought a plane ticket. Just four days before you died. Where were you going? The thing that itches in his brain unfurls pale, gelid tendrils, coils them around its fat, glistening lobes.

He makes a telephone call to Rueda, and Rueda in turn makes a series of calls to other people. A day passes, two days, three. On the fourth day Rueda calls back. The flight was headed to General Santos City on the morning of December 31. But the ticket wasn't for Libby, it was for an Evangeline de Vera.

EV.

"Do we know who she is?"

"My people are checking."

"Call me when you know. Oh, and Mike . . . ?"

"Yes, Father?"

"We need to know if de Vera made that flight, and if she's back in Manila. And if not—we want her back."

The first time it happens, she surprises herself. She finds herself telling the woman sitting across from her (*colleague, twenty-six, married two years, miscarried once because of the beatings*) that she'll help. The words come out before she can censor them, before she can think about the implications. She lays down the ground rules, making them up as she goes along, realizing only much later that they make perfect sense. *Don't call him, don't meet with him in person, don't tell him where you are. Communicate only through your lawyer, the lawyer I'm going to introduce you to, he's a good man.* She lets the woman stay at the house in Lagro for a few weeks; when the time is right, she sends her away to a relative in another city, someone the woman trusts.

It's more than a year later when she receives word of the annulment from the woman herself; a telephone call, exhausted but happy, and so very grateful. It's a long conversation. After she hangs up, she breaks open a bottle of wine, puts on some

Cole Porter—the *Classic Cole* album by Jan DeGaetani—and dances slowly in the living room in her bare feet.

It happens again, once, twice, word gets around. She forks out her own money, and if she doesn't have enough, she works the telephone and writes e-mails, she calls in favors, asks a few trusted friends. She seems to know instinctively how to do this, she becomes an expert, she could write a manual. She falls into it as though she were meant to do it, born to do it, weaving it seamlessly into the fabric of her life.

When her father dies, the relatives ask her to please come. She refuses but she says, *Send me the urn*. When it arrives, she drives to a rundown gas station along Regalado Avenue, heads for the restroom, locks the door. She empties the contents of the urn into a filthy toilet bowl and flushes them down the drain. And flushes. And flushes. And flushes.

The woman who knocks on Saenz's door is in her fifties, short and plump and well dressed. He immediately pegs her for a teacher. He signals her to come in with a wave of his hand.

She seems nervous, and Saenz reminds himself to be gentle. *You remember how that goes, don't you?*

She is Professor Josephine Atienza, one of Libby's former teachers at the University of the Philippines. She says she read in the papers that Saenz was helping with the investigation. The words tumble out one after another, she keeps talking even as she roots around in her handbag for something. There's a certain desperation in her speech and her actions, as though she must get this business in his office exactly right.

When the professor finds the slip of paper she's looking for, she pulls it out and hands it to Saenz.

"Libby came to my office just after Christmas. She said she urgently needed a place to stay in GenSan. I was born and raised there, so she came to me. A short-term stay of a month or two. I asked her why GenSan of all places, and she said she was working on a project." Professor Atienza taps the paper with her forefinger. "That's the place I recommended."

Saenz studies the paper for a moment, then looks up at the professor. "She lied to you," he tells her.

Anger flickers in her eyes but it's quickly replaced by resignation, and she swallows down whatever she may have been thinking of saying. "Libby never lied. She just left out the truth."

The woman's husband is Korean, and he is something of a sexual sadist. She wears a scarf at her throat, the bruises fading now from ugly purple to mottled yellow. She tries to explain the things he does to her in the bedroom, but she can't quite find the words because nothing in her life before him has prepared her for this, for the kind of assault he inflicts, for the level of filth he subjects her to; she has no vocabulary for it. She looks about ready to crawl out of her skin.

Libby sits back and listens to the woman try to tell her story in between great, wracking sobs. At some point, she looks out the window, at the trees beyond. She hasn't tuned out; she's just hearing the story in another woman's voice. After a while, all these women tell their stories in that same voice.

Saenz used to think that when he got to this age, sleep would come more easily. Not true; or perhaps, just not true for him. He cannot remember the last time he slept seven or eight hours straight, it seems an impossible luxury. He stays awake for long stretches, sometimes longer than twenty-four hours. When he finally collapses from exhaustion, his mind struggles mightily against the tide of sleep. He snaps awake in an hour or less. It takes him another hour or two to fall asleep again, and the cycle starts over. He's always so tired, it's become an agony to put one foot in front of the other every day. Some days he feels tethered to the earth by the leaden weight of his own aging body, and he prays for release.

It's been several months now since they found Libby Delgado. Every day that passes, the man who killed her slips farther away from their grasp. Lab tests, requests for information, paperwork, everything moves slowly, as it always does in Manila. Rueda tries his best, he always does, that's why Saenz likes him, but the system is what it is, it's like swimming in cold porridge. The DNA, the hair, the fingerprints don't match anything on record, but given the state of record-keeping in the country, it was always going to be a long shot.

She pulls him into her gravity every night, even though there's nothing left of her but a few handfuls of ash in a marble jar somewhere. *Who are you?* he rasps out when he wakes from his fragmented dreams, his uneasy sleep. He reaches for his cell phone, he can't help it, he's drawn to those eyes, so very angry, so very alive in her dead face.

The ground rules are clear. *No direct contact with him. Always through a lawyer, or the police if necessary.* It is the First Rule, a kind of detox to break his hold on the woman's mind and will. It gives her a chance to see through all the little tricks calculated to make her feel small and defective and unworthy. It forces her to start hearing her own voice and thinking her own thoughts again.

The Second Rule is: *If you break the First Rule, you never tell him where you are.*

From the pension house on Pioneer Street in GenSan, Rueda's people manage to trace Evangeline de Vera to the home of a cousin in the same city. They bring her back to Metro Manila, and all the while she demands to know why. When they tell her, she is utterly stunned, she had no idea. She has had no access to Manila newspapers these last few months, and her cousin's family doesn't watch the news on television.

She and Libby had little in common, don't move in the same circles. Evangeline is in her late twenties, tiny, blandly pretty. Barely got past high school. Used to work as a waitress at a karaoke joint, where she met the Korean businessman she eventually married. She has no children, no job.

Rueda asks Evangeline how she met Libby, why the older woman would buy a plane ticket in her name and pay for it with her own credit card. She says she hadn't known Libby very long, and she doesn't remember how they met. But she insists they were friends; she was short of cash for a trip she needed to make to see her family, and Libby was kind enough to lend her money for a flight and accommodations.

"But you're married. Why didn't you just ask your husband for the money instead?" Rueda probes.

Both the inspector and the priest—one inside the room, the other watching the exchange from outside—are quick to notice the brief moment of hesitation.

"He was . . . out of town." She won't look directly at Rueda. "Traveling."

Unnecessary, Saenz thinks. *People add unnecessary emphasis or detail when they're lying.*

When they take a break, Rueda asks him, "What if it's true? What if that's really all there is, and we're wasting our time?"

Saenz holds up both hands in exasperation. "She can't—won't—tell us how she met Libby. Who introduced them. Exactly how long they've known each other. Why she couldn't ask her husband for the money. She's being evasive. She's terrified."

On a hunch, he asks Rueda to bring him Libby's planner and

the clothes they found near the washing machine at her house. When they arrive, both men go back into the room where Evangeline is waiting. Rueda introduces the priest. The tension that ripples through her small frame is unmistakable.

Saenz sits across from her, and Rueda takes a seat in the corner.

The priest does not ask her questions. Instead, he tells her a story—her story—in his low, quiet voice, reading off dates and entries on the planner. He tells her that she met Libby at her office on the 28th of October last year. Someone named Gemma introduced them. They met again several times, without Gemma, but never again at Libby's office, always in a public place—a fast-food joint, a café, a park.

He tells her that she met Libby three times at a hospital, first in late November and twice in December. He says that Evangeline was either sick or injured—the entries in Libby's planner switched from *meet* to *visit* the first two times, and to *pick up* on the third. He tells her gently that it would be relatively easy for the police to check on the circumstances of these hospitalizations. He tells her that Libby booked the flight and paid for it four days after *pick up EV from hosp*.

Evangeline is gripping the armrests of her chair so hard that her knuckles jut sharp and white through the skin of her hands.

Saenz draws the clothes out of the plastic bag they came in. "These are yours," he says, laying them on the table and pushing them across to her. "You stayed with her after you were discharged from the hospital. You left them to dry in the guest bathroom when you flew off to GenSan."

She reaches out and touches them.

"He found them," Saenz tells her quietly, sadly. "It made him angry."

"He couldn't have," she protests, confirming his theory without even realizing it. "How could he . . . Oh, God." There it is, the horror of it, coming to her now in all its unforgiving clarity. "I called him. She told me not to, but I thought it would . . . calm him down."

"And you told him where you were staying," the priest says.

Evangeline de Vera, breaking Libby's rules. "Oh, God. Was it because of me? Was it my fault?"

The two men don't answer. To Evangeline, that's answer enough.

Libby always makes it a point to lock herself away on New Year's Eve, because she can't stand the noise and the smoke. It's easier to do it in the Lagro house, up on a hill, and even though the neighbors will be setting off fireworks and drinking and generally making fools of themselves, their homes are far enough apart that she doesn't really have to suffer through any of it. She plans her own private celebration with a tub of Magnolia ice cream in the fridge and a few action films on DVD.

She is about to lock the gate when the car drives up. As the man steps out, she immediately knows who he is and why he is here.

Libby knows that it isn't wise to engage him; he's calm now but she senses his anger, it's coming off him in waves. Quickly she estimates how long it's been since Evangeline's plane took off. *Twelve hours, that's enough time if she follows instructions.*

But she hasn't, which is why he's here. And Libby thinks she might be able to buy Evangeline a little more time, so she shakes his hand, invites him in for coffee and some of those *rosquillos* that a colleague at the bank brought her from Cebu.

Before they go into the house, she steals a look at the night sky. Between the New Year's Eve fireworks and the smoke now hanging heavy over the city, she can't see a single star.

The police have learned that Hann Hyun-jun fled the country less than a week after Libby Delgado's murder. They've matched samples of his hair and fingerprints from the condo unit he'd shared with Evangeline to the samples found in Libby's house. But there's little that can be done other than to get Interpol to put out a red notice for him and wait. He has money, though, and he could go anywhere. Rueda tells Saenz there's no way to predict how soon, or if, he will ever be found.

The priest continues to reconstruct Libby Delgado out of Evangeline de Vera's recollections, out of the connections that are now emerging from their association. They web out into the lives of other women—Fanny Jamora, Astrid Samaniego, Lisa Marie Borja . . . The list spans eight years, five cities, thirteen lives—nineteen if he counts the children. She took it all on herself, led by some impulse that even now eludes him.

She's left him with little to go on, and there's no family history to be found anywhere in the silent house on Caridad Street. But Saenz is patient, he wants to know—to understand her life and the magnitude of what she's done.

Professor Atienza meets him at the Starbucks café at the huge new SM Fairview mall along Quirino Avenue. She insists on buying him coffee (his usual double-shot espresso, not helping the insomnia) and chooses for herself the sweetest, richest concoction on the menu, three hundred tablespoons of sugar and a half-pound of whipped cream. "Life is short," she declares. She giggles like a schoolgirl, guilty and defiant at the same time.

It's different when they're settled at a table; they sit in silence for several minutes, as if bracing themselves for what's to come. "You knew, didn't you?" he finally asks. "When you came to my office. You knew who was staying at the pension house in GenSan."

Tears well up in her eyes, and she fiercely blinks them away. "I didn't know who. But I knew why."

Saenz leans forward, his pale, fine-boned hands clasped together between his knees. In his mind, Libby's eyes slowly lose their anger, her face relaxing into the easy, barely-there smile in the photographs that are not on his mobile phone.

"Tell me," he says.

THE PROFESSOR'S WIFE

BY JOSE DALISAY

Diliman

Somebody died in this car I'm driving. That's why I got it so cheap. I mean, new Ford Escapes don't go for less than a million pesos, and even discounting a few years' use—five years, to be exact, and fifty-two thousand kilometers on the odometer—I'd have valued this 4x2 XLS at around 530,000, maybe even a bit more in those used-car lots that have sprung up everywhere around Metro Manila, near the malls to catch the dads' eyes while the moms shop. But 365,000? That's a steal. That's robbery. Unless you figure all the scrubbing it took to get the blood off the upholstery in the back, right behind me where the professor's head would have been, the blood bubbling out of his mouth and his nostrils and who knows what other cavities. His wife's lap would have caught some if not most of the blood, but I could just imagine that head, that whole upper frame of his, jerking up and down like some broken insect, spewing blood and mucus all over the car seat. Of course I didn't really see any blood when I looked—not that I looked too closely—because the seats sported new beige velour covers when I got the car, and I couldn't smell anything either because the wife—Lalaine, that's her name, I keep calling her Mrs. Sanvictores, or Ma'am Lalaine, never just "Lalaine" to her face or in the professor's presence—had sprayed a canful of acrid-sweet lemon air-freshener into the interior.

How did I learn about the way the professor died? From

Lalaine, of course, she was there, cradling his bony head on her ample lap where he might have, would have, lain the same birdlike head—I remember how, when he nodded in class, it almost seemed like he was pecking, the way his nose would dip forward and then pull back—some other time, any other time. Heck, I'll admit, I would have too with half a chance, and given how I'd sometimes steal a glance at that lap—and, oh, at other parts of Mrs. Sanvictores, or Lalaine. It wasn't my fault; it was the professor himself who invited me into his house, their house, to discuss his research on the origins of the coffee industry on Sibutu Island—and I didn't even know he had a wife, or a young wife to be exact, a hot young wife who must have been thirty years his junior, and maybe just ten years older than I was, if even that much.

The second I met Lalaine, as she bent over to hand me a glass of pineapple juice and all kinds of good things began to spill out of the front of her low-cut blouse, I nearly fainted from the sight and the whiff of Shalimar or whatever they name those perfumes that remind you of rustling silk and moonlight. The truth is, she wasn't what you would call particularly pretty—her cheekbones seemed set a bit too high and the sides of her face tapered down so sharply into her nubbin of a chin that you could've said she looked like a caricature, especially with those full wide lips. She was a walking, bobbing exaggeration of a woman, or womanhood itself, that's what I always thought. Her skin was so white and creamy that the large brown mole that sat on the hump of her left breast looked even larger and browner than it probably was.

"You didn't even ask if he wanted Coke instead of pineapple juice," the professor chided his wife as she bent at the knees, with the practiced dip of a professional dancer, to serve my drink.

"This is better for his health," she retorted in a Tagalog that resonated with provincial charm, making me imagine tender papayas, broiling squid, and potent rum, or whatever they drink down there, south of Tablas Strait.

"It's all right, I prefer juice." I practically grabbed the drink from her hand. When my fingers grazed hers I felt like I had been scorched, like the juice would vaporize.

Indeed, it seemed like a fine mist had crept into the afternoon, and as we sat there in the professor's garden, with him droning on about Leandro de Veana's report to the Crown about exploiting the colony's natural resources, I watched Lalaine's shadow through the jalousies, puttering about in the kitchen, maybe making little rice cakes. That's what I often imagined her doing, I don't know why, they just seemed to go together, Lalaine and rice cakes. I'll bet she made a lot of them for the professor.

My reverie was broken when the buzzer rang at the gate—it was Dencio, a handyman who lived in the squatters' settlement nearby, in Krus na Ligas. They used him as a gardener, a plumber, a carpenter, and sometimes even a driver, when they had functions to attend and the professor didn't want to crease his *barong* by driving the Ford Escape himself. Dencio was one of those hard-luck characters, the guy who works his butt off fixing other people's problems but who can't shake off his own. The professor told me that Dencio had been all set to fly to a construction job in Dubai when his youngest daughter fell ill with dengue after a mosquito bite, and died. Then his wife went insane with grief and walked into the path of a dump truck, leaving him with five kids to feed, one of whom has encephalitis. I mean, who writes these scripts? Now here he was to repair—he announced to me when I opened the gate for him—a leak in the septic tank. A big job, Dencio muttered, both of his pudgy hands clutching large, heavy tools to break the earth with.

So that's where the vague stink was coming from. I know, I didn't mention it earlier, but I was thinking of Lalaine—Shalimar, remember?—and had shut out the creeping suggestion of decay, something that now afflicted me with cloying tartness, now that Dencio had mentioned it and Lalaine was out of sight. Or rather, she had stepped out for a second to let Dencio into the main house and into the backyard, where the septic tank was located. She looked happy to see him, and murmured something I couldn't understand—I think they came from the same part of the country and spoke the same dialect—and for a minute back there I wondered if Dencio looked at Lalaine the same way I did. It seemed like a silly idea. Men with five kids to feed don't have time to fantasize, do they? Now the stink was definitely in the air, like the earth's own bad breath. Even the professor noticed it, not that he minded too much. "Sometimes a dead bird falls on the roof," he said, although I wondered how he could have known that, and how large and dead a bird had to be to create such rot. But I could believe how the roofs of these faculty houses might accumulate all kinds of garbage, even as the professor and I spoke; and on other visits, our conversation would be interrupted by the thud of a falling mango from one of the stout branches arching over the property.

Let me tell you about these old houses on the UP campus. They were built in the '50s and some of them still have the suburban look of that time, where they pinched the wet concrete for cheap texture and carved the outlines of rocks and boulders on the wall before painting the pebbled spaces over, just to offset the basic gray boxiness of the house itself. They had given the professor one of these, a concrete shell that he began to fill with books of every imaginable kind, including obscure commentaries on the apocalypse, herbal recipes for the relief of gout, and a pictorial history of the American Civil War.

I can imagine Professor Sanvictores coming to UP as a young instructor, eager to make his mark in history. Or was it economics that he first signed up for? This was years before his stint as a teaching assistant and doctoral candidate in Minnesota, where he picked up and cultivated the American accent that many coeds found charming, if not irresistible. Now every two-bit club and radio deejay and call center agent has one, but none of them can come up with and use a word like "contumacious" the way the professor did to describe certain tribal chieftains in old New Zealand.

I was dying to ask either the professor or Lalaine herself how the two of them met, and more than that, how they ended up being man and wife. I mean, what ever did they see in each other? But of course, silly, I knew what he saw in *her*, I could see that even with my eyes shut. But what about Lalaine? I could understand her developing a schoolgirl crush on him, especially if he put on that Minnesota affect and gave his sophomore-class version of his lecture on Rizal's women and free love in the nineteenth century. Truth be told, in his younger days the professor might have been found attractive by some women from a certain angle, especially women who liked stray cats and boys with cowlicks and otherwise smart men who needed to be helped with the simplest things, like using an ATM card. And did the professor have any money? It's a fair thing to ask. From what I'd gathered—and I would hear this again at the wake, not that too many family members bothered to show up—there had been a farm in Quezon Province, somewhere on that long, ragged, storm-bitten eastern shore nobody really wants to call home. The professor's mother had wanted him to become a priest; his father a lawyer or a businessman. Both parents expected their only son to get married, but they died long before Lalaine stepped into his life—or did he step into hers?

Almost as soon as Lalaine appeared beside the professor on campus, the predictable gossip swirled about her being a bargirl he'd met during a semester spent doing research down south, maybe while he was trying to figure out how the plague that ravaged Brazil's coffee industry reached Sibutu's liberica plantations in 1888. Nobody thought to ask Lalaine for her CV, or they assumed she was some graduate assistant like me. Even at the wake, nobody thought to ask her sensible questions like, *So have you thought of donating his papers to the university archives?* or, *Isn't it wonderful that Professor Umali came to pay his respects?* If there was anyone who would have wanted the professor dead, it was Calixto Umali. He had been a thorn in the professor's side for ages—at one time, his protégé, like me, and then his rival and archcritic, especially after he'd returned with his PhD from Leipzig—you know, where Goethe, Wagner, and Nietzsche all wore the school jersey—taking every opportunity to dispute the professor's theories and gathering his own coterie of departmental groupies around him, the kind with braces on their teeth. Umali cut quite a figure as well, with a full shock of hair, like a crown. Sometimes I think the professor brought Lalaine back from Sibutu and married her—cake, bouquet, pigeon, and all— just to prove that he knew something more about life than migration theories and why empires crumble.

And then when he bought the Ford Escape—in a color the dealers call "toreador red"—the professor looked even younger, snappier, more eager to engage anyone in anything, from a debate at the University Council to a drag race on Temple Drive. Or so it seemed. I was still a senior then and his baby-thesis advisee, not yet his assistant, but he had made it a point to ask me to join him in the SUV for a ride to the post office, using a supposed problem with my endnotes to Chapter 6, on the Battle of Biak-na-Bato, as an excuse. As soon as we were driving down A. Roces Street, nothing about my thesis was ever brought up again. Instead, he told me about how he'd cashed in some stocks he had inherited a long time ago from his father to buy the car—

his retirement paycheck was still too far away—and that the Escape was his wedding gift to himself and Lalaine. One of these
days, he said, he'd teach her how to drive, but not too soon.
Heck, maybe it was better to get her a driver, he added. Lalaine
was bound to scratch the car up, she was good with dainty little
things like cups and saucers, but large objects confounded her,
she was new to all this and an SUV was just too much. It was
at this point that I wanted to ask him how they had met, but
we had reached the post office, and the professor realized with
a chuckle that he had forgotten the parcel he was supposed to
send his sister in Chicago. "I know, they're all wondering why I
married her, asking who and what she is, like it's their business,"
he muttered as we drove back to the faculty center. "But if you
were me, you'd do the same thing, I'm sure you would." I kept
quiet, but I wanted to say, *Of course, professor, I certainly would,
I'm your man, whatever is good for you is good for me too!*

And so it went for a few years, during which I graduated
with my degree in history. I thought I would go on to law school
and realize my father's dream of having an attorney in the family.
For a brief while I even got a job as a call center agent, advis-
ing people in Ohio how to set up their digital answering ma-
chines, only to keep returning to campus and hanging out with
the professor. Eventually I signed up for an MA. I didn't really
see myself becoming an academic or a professional historian—I
mean, I loved all the war stories, the expeditions and encounters
with strange tribes, that sort of thing. But the kind of history the
professor was seriously interested in, having to do with varieties
of coffee beans and price fluctuations in Antwerp and Rio de
Janeiro, was almost like Accounting 312 to me. I suppose I was
fascinated by the professor and by his young wife, and by the life
they led. I'd expected her to get pregnant within months of their
wedding, but it never happened. I got used to seeing Lalaine just

the way she was, just short of pregnant. Me, I'd had a couple of girlfriends, nothing serious. I was never good at figuring out what they wanted, except the obvious, which turned out to be something they didn't really want as much as I did. I mean, what is it with these women? It's not like I grope or fondle them the first chance I get. I do everything by the book—saving up for dates so I can take them to a decent dinner after the movie, telling them about my day and asking about theirs, escorting them home in a cab and being properly hesitant when they ask me in, focusing on the TV while they make coffee, keeping my hands on my knees until they relax and get that glassy look in their eyes, talking about future and family. I start feeling frisky and touch them somewhere that seems to burn, because they jump up and say things I never had in mind, and I go home totally bummed out. I hate to say this because I dislike generalizations, although history tells us that when you take a really long step backward and look again, people tend to do the same basic things wherever they are, whether in China in the Qing dynasty or in Montezuma's Mexico, but I came around to the conclusion that it was my not having a car, my own car, at the age of twenty-four, that made me look not so hot to the girls. I mean, let's face it, driving a car makes you look like you can do anything, or go anywhere—even the professor knew that. I'm sure those Egyptian charioteers got laid a whole lot more than the foot soldiers, the cowboys more than the cooks. I'd brought this up with my parents—I still lived with them in Kamuning and drove the old man around in his '93 Civic that now coughed in first gear and groaned in second. It was hard to convince sixty-somethings that they, *I*, needed a new car when their only son was a perpetual schoolboy, earning little beyond the scraps the professor threw me from his research funding and the transcription jobs I took on now and then for other academics. (Once, even, in a really bad fix, from Professor

Umali himself. Although of course it had to be kept secret, and I swear I never broke any confidences or passed along any gossip.)

Luckily—okay, it's hardly the word, considering the circumstances, but you know what I mean—my dad was close to retirement, and fairly susceptible to suggestions of spending his golden years driving or being driven around the country, like to weekends in Tagaytay or Subic with my mom. And I just had to appeal to his sense of entitlement to get him to agree that he deserved a prize for all his decades of hard work in the maritime insurance industry. That was the key—it was going to be *his* car, not mine. That way he would also pay for the gas and the spark plugs, even if he was going to stay home most of the time playing Scrabble with my mom. When the 2005 Ford Escape came up for sale at that unbelievably low price, all I had to do was give Dad a little nudge for him to tip over and sign the check, hallelujah. It was like the heavens had conspired to deliver me a chariot in toreador red, to reward me for my cleverness, and to compensate me for all the nasty rejections I'd received since high school.

But this isn't about me or the car. It's the professor I'm talking about, isn't it? . . . about how he died that awful day in late November.

Some time in September, things began to go wrong, horribly wrong, for the professor. It was bad enough that Typhoon Emong hit the country, the strongest and worst in nearly thirty years. Which was longer than I'd been alive, come to think of it. Emong killed hundreds of people as far south as Surigao, and brought crusty old trees crashing down on power lines, so that the UP campus went without light and water for three days. I rode a bike to the professor's house just to see how they were doing, and found the old man drying out some papers. Letters from his mother, he said—written while he was still in graduate school—that had been soaked when the wind ripped off a corner of the roof and rain came streaming in. I was surprised to hear the roof creaking and see Lalaine up there herself, hammer in hand, tamping down the errant sheet of galvanized iron. I shouted to her and she acknowledged me with a wave. Looking up at her in shorts, I caught a glimpse of long white thigh before Lalaine disappeared to work on the dangerous edge and I had a chance to say, "Be careful."

But like I said, worse things were to come for the professor.

First, a few days after the storm lifted and the last fallen branches had been cleared by road crews, Professor Sanvictores came home dejected, profoundly humiliated by Professor Umali's incontrovertible proof that the annual reports to the governor-general from his caretaker in Sibutu had been outright forgeries or fatally compromised copies—at least the segments from 1885 to 1891—given that the real records had been unearthed by one of Umali's assistants at the Houghton Library in Harvard. Professor Sanvictores was so upset and distracted, he scraped the left fender guard of the Escape against a post in the garage entry-way when he drove home. It's still there, a faint and meaningless scratch, more annoying than anything, but there.

Second, Lalaine had become pregnant by someone else. The professor told me the somber news in mid-November, while we were sitting under the mango tree that shaded the gazebo in the yard. His face was in the shadows: "But I couldn't get it up. I never could," he said. "That was the problem, that was *our* problem."

Lalaine had tearfully confessed to a liaison with Dencio. I felt outraged, like I myself had been betrayed—like I said, how could a man with five mouths to feed think of carrying on with another man's wife? I had come to the professor's house to pick up my salary for the past two months' work. I usually got paid monthly, and never complained. But when the old man handed me my check, his hand trembling in grief, I felt so embarrassed, so sorry for him, that I almost gave it back, as if I myself had something to feel guilty about.

"What will you do now?" I asked in a voice that sounded even weaker than his.

"I don't know," he said. "For some strange reason, I want to keep the baby, but not keep her. God forgive me for saying this, but sometimes I just want to strangle Lalaine in her sleep, and then I remember that it was me who asked her to come here and live with me and my books, to cook for me and occupy half of my bed, all of which and more she's done without complaint. And when I remember that, much of the pain goes away, at least until I wake up and see her, or hear her mumbling something in that dialect of hers, and suddenly she becomes a horrible stranger again . . . And then I too become someone else, someone I don't want to know." He raised his hands and spread his spindly fingers out in what might have been a profession of innocence, or surrender, or he could have been pushing something back, I don't know, and he hung his head down in silence, like he was praying, but I didn't think he was.

"I'm sorry to hear that" was all I could say. The professor said nothing, and to break the awkwardness of the moment, I excused myself to go to the bathroom.

For over a week before the storm, Dencio had been digging out a large pit in the back for a new septic tank. The old one was beyond repair and foul brown sludge had begun bubbling up in the toilet. I saw that myself when I went in for a pee. Lalaine had done what she could to contain the overflow with rolled-up newspapers, but I could see how, despite her best efforts, the house was beginning to be less habitable by the day. The professor's books and papers filled every shelf and cranny like an overgrown garden with the shrubbery gone mad. A small altar was tucked away in a corner with glowing electric bulbs illuminating Jesus cradling his heart in his palm. It had to be hers, because I never knew the professor to be a churchgoing man. I mean, the word

"God" would sometimes creep into his speech, like an expression, and I know enough about social scientists to know that when they say "God," it's with all kinds of little asterisks.

That's when I saw her in a corner of the kitchen, as I stepped out of the bathroom, breathless because I had stopped inhaling the instant I noticed all those soggy newspapers on the floor. I actually heard her before I saw her—whimpering in a chair, with her knees up and her arms curled around them. She looked up—surprised, embarrassed, defiant, fearful—and it occurred to me that we had never really spoken about anything more serious than the weather or her rice cakes, certainly not in private. Through the window, I could see that the professor was still in the gazebo, maintaining a stoic silence, flipping through the pages of a newspaper like he cared about what was happening in Afghanistan. Lalaine sat backlit, so that her edges seemed even softer, silvered in shadow. I could see the wetness of her nose, and when she noticed me standing there, she abruptly brushed the snot with the back of her hand. It only made things worse by smearing her cheek, but somehow Lalaine looked vulnerable and therefore all the more beautiful to me.

"Are you all right?" I instantly realized the stupidity of my question.

"Help me," I thought I heard her say, and moved closer so I could be sure. "My husband's going to kill me." She began rocking herself and crying. "He can't forgive me, he's going to kill me, I just know it."

"No," I said, not even sure why. "The professor wouldn't hurt anyone, especially not you."

She looked up sharply. "You're not his wife. How would you know?"

I felt like snapping back with, *You're not his wife, either,* or something to that effect, just to register my own disgust about how she'd betrayed the man. She and Dencio, she *with* Dencio.

"You have no idea the things he makes me do. I do them to keep him happy, because I promised to love him. And I don't care if you believe me or not, but I still do."

"Then why would he kill you? And if you think he will, why don't you leave? You should go home." My voice was laced with bitterness and chastisement, and I realized that I might as well have been speaking for the professor.

"I have no other home," she said. "There was another man, back in Sibutu. He was an evil man, he hurt me. I came here to get away from him. But everything," she sighed, "everything just gets worse and worse."

My mind reeled. How many other men did this woman have in her life, and how could I believe all the stories she was telling me about them? And granted, she must have been woefully unlucky to shack up with the wrong guys. But how about taking some responsibility for her own poor choices, and for whatever she might have done to make good men go bad? I mean, history, folks, history—Jezebel, Delilah, Cleopatra, Mata Hari, it's a list that just goes on and on.

"Well, that's true," I said. "You can't keep running away from the past." If there was anything I learned from school, anything at all, it was that.

Apparently sensing my lack of sympathy, Lalaine rose up from her chair to get a glass of water and gave me a steely, almost reptilian glance that simply confirmed my own dawning mistrust of Mrs. Sanvictores. Or whoever she really was. How could all that liquid softness vanish so quickly, and be replaced by this new skin, hard, resistant, and opaque?

I noticed through the jalousies that the professor had left the gazebo. I wondered if he had observed my brief exchange with his wife, or whatever she was to him now. Suddenly the thought crossed my mind that he might have—could have, should have—suspected me of being the baby's father at some point, if she hadn't fingered Dencio. I mean, it was possible, wasn't it? As far as I could tell, apart from the professor himself and that sneaky Dencio, I was the only male who went into their house with any kind of frequency. Never mind that Lalaine and I hardly ever spoke. I could have gotten her cell phone number and initiated and carried on an affair via text, beginning with innocuous thanks and comments about the refreshments, and then about the decor, or her perfume, raising the level of intimacy with every message. That's what I could have done but never did, and meanwhile this half-literate handyman was giving it to her by the bucket, while I listened to the professor deliver the annual Cesar Adib Majul Memorial Lecture at the C. M. Recto Hall and chased coffee production figures at the National Library.

"I have to go back to the professor," I told Lalaine, who had turned away from me, which was just as well because she now seemed ugly to me, even her legs where I could see splotchy patches, maybe from all the tension and the guilt. "I'm sure you'll be all right." Now that she was standing upright, up to her full height that nearly matched mine, she hardly seemed the helpless victim of moments before.

I couldn't find the professor anywhere in the front garden, so I went out back. There he was, staring into the yawning pit that Dencio had dug for the new septic tank. How was this ever going to get finished, I wondered, now that the professor knew about the affair and Dencio had presumably been fired? The pit had filled to the brim with rainwater during the storm, but the waters had subsided and I could see the hole was large and deep enough to swallow a man, the soft rough edges of its mouth making a silent scream of warning.

"In Herculaneum," the professor said, "they excavated tons of compacted human waste from a septic tank, and so were able to establish what the citizens ate, like dormice and sea urchins. It's funny how we learn about people from the shit they leave behind."

That was the last time I saw the professor alive—at least literally speaking, since the following day I heard him, through the partly open door of his faculty center office, speaking to none other than Professor Umali. I couldn't make out exactly what they were saying—and the fear suddenly seized me that it was about my perfidy in having worked for Umali a few years earlier. I began constructing my tortured defense—then realized that they were having a casual conversation, almost as if Calixto Umali was back to being the professor's most brilliant and respectful pupil. One of these days I'll ask Umali about that unexpected visit, like who called whom first and what was on the agenda. I might even wheedle some work from him again, and feel guilt-free now that the professor's gone, but we'll see.

Two mornings later I got a text from Jo-Anne, our departmental secretary, telling me that the professor had died. *What, where, how, why?* I texted back quickly. I'd just come out of the shower and hadn't even pulled my pants on—but even before Jo-Anne responded, a flurry of ideas ran through my mind. Chiefly, that Lalaine somehow had something to do with his death. At the very least, she had driven him to it.

Jo-Anne's text seemed to confirm my suspicions: *Accidental fall into hole behind house. Hit head.* That was no simple hole, that was the septic tank, and yes you could lose your footing on the edge, fall in, and hit your head on the hollow-block floor and get a nasty bump, but it wouldn't kill you—it just didn't look deep enough—unless you were hit again and again.

I could just see it happening: Lalaine luring the professor to the backyard, then Dencio coming from behind with a shovel and whacking the old man over the head with it, jumping into the pit to slug the professor some more and finish the job. I was sure that Lalaine had texted Dencio, then given him that *Help, he's going to kill me* look, and that Dencio quickly figured out the side benefits of compassion and had mustered the temerity to do her bidding. But if they'd killed the old man there, why not just leave his body in the pit and cover it with earth and concrete? Too obvious; I'd often noticed Lalaine watching those true-crime and *CSI*-type shows on TV, where the scheming wife and her lover-accomplice always get caught. "The soil's too fresh," the detective would always mutter, pawing on bent knees at an obviously off-color spot.

"We drove him to the hospital," Lalaine told me that same afternoon, in the very same gazebo where I had been sitting with the professor just two days earlier. I had to go to that house, I had to hear it from her own mouth, I wanted to see Lalaine twitch and hear her sputter, trying to explain away the terrible truth. "It happened late last night, around one a.m. I woke up to get a glass of water, I'm always thirsty being pregnant, and he was gone from his bed—actually the sofa in the living room, where he now sleeps, or was now sleeping . . . Anyway, the door was open and I looked out and—I don't know how, but I could feel where he was, what he was doing or wanted to do. So I took a flashlight and went to the backyard, calling his name, but there was no answer. And when I looked into that hole in the ground he was already there, unconscious, bleeding. I jumped in to try and pull him out, but I couldn't . . . so I called Dencio."

"*Dencio?* Why not call me? I'm sure you have my number somewhere."

"There was no time to look. Dencio lives close by, and I was very afraid. He came, rushed right over, and helped me pull my poor husband out of the pit, and we brought him to Labor Hospital but it was too late. He died in my arms, in the back of the car. You know—he was still alive when I found him."

I didn't know where to begin tearing away at her lies. Dead from a fall into a six-foot pit? Okay, sure. Dencio so conveniently nearby? So, all right, Krus na Ligas was just five minutes away on a bike, but why not scream to call the neighbors for help, like genuinely distraught wives are supposed to do? Driving to Labor Hospital? Why not the UP infirmary just a few streets away—not that they were good for much more than dispensing Tylenol? Again, why drive anywhere at all? Why not just let their victim writhe to his death at the bottom of that infernal pit? Perhaps she suffered a pang of guilt watching him lie there, looking back at her with *How could you?* in his glazed-over eyes. Did Dencio drive the Ford Escape at full speed, or did he take his time cruising out of the UP gates and onto C. P. Garcia, maybe stopping for a burger in a twenty-four-hour McDonald's along the way?

And now that I gazed at Lalaine in her proper widow's somber dress, a deep-blue linen outfit with a modest neckline that she might have worn to a dinner with other faculty wives at the Executive House had she felt up to it, I didn't know whether to marvel at, or be appalled by, her incredible composure. Her simple words were inflected with emotion and what I had mistaken for sweet naïveté, that's how dangerous she was. I realized that this was going to be a bit more difficult case to crack, that I had to be equally deft and skillful in probing the mind and motives of the widow Sanvictores.

It was the audacity of her next gambit that astounded me. Placing her hand so carefully that her fingertips just barely touched my knee, and with no suggestion of malice or enticement in her demeanor whatsoever, the widow Sanvictores glanced at the parked Escape and asked: "Would you like to buy my husband's car? I need to go away for a while and could use the cash. I just realized I have very little money, and it will take time to go through his papers. You understand, of course—about the car, all the memories. I don't drive, and . . . and I know you like it. I've seen how you look at it."

My throat went dry. Of course she had seen me look, many times, at the car, at herself. Unlike my girlfriends, she knew what I wanted, and was prepared to give it, at least in stages. "I don't have much money," I began to whine. "I'm just a graduate student, and the Escape is such a nice car." She or someone— maybe Dencio?—had taken the trouble to wash the SUV that morning, so that it sparkled more than usual, enough to give me a headache. But I managed to pull myself together and pop the question: "How much do you want for it? Maybe my father can help. He needs a new car, or a newer one, anyway." I covered my mouth with my hand to disguise my desperation.

She beamed and picked up a pencil from the gazebo table— I could see lots of numbers on a pad of paper, so she must've been working on some calculations when I called to say I was coming by—and wrote a number: 365. The buzz in my head got stronger. Surely this was a mistake. Didn't she know how much a 2005 Ford Escape XLS was worth? Had she even bothered to ask around or bought one of those car magazines at the pharmacy checkout for thirty pesos, scanned the ads, and realized she could make herself an extra hundred thousand or two? I know; I've looked. I buy those magazines and dream about Audis and Alfa Romeos, but that's because I'm a regular guy.

"Are you sure?" I asked.

"I'm a simple woman," Lalaine said. "I just want a quick sale. I'm sure your dear father can help—but if you don't want the car, Dencio probably knows people who—"

"No!" I said. "Not Dencio. Look, I want the car. Give me a day or two. I'll talk to my father. Three hundred sixty-five? Consider it sold."

She glanced at the SUV again, wistfully, then smiled at me. "This is a very sad day. I've lost my husband. They're moving his body to the University Chapel, and I will be going there later to join him. I came home just to change and—and because you called to say you were dropping by. You make me very happy by . . . helping me recover. Thank you. We have a deal." She took both of my hands in hers and pressed them, just long enough to send over a surge of warmth. "Let me get the keys so you can take it for a drive. And maybe you can drive me to the chapel, no? We can pay our respects to someone we both loved, you and I."

I could hear birds singing in the mango trees.

Like I said, somebody died in this car I'm driving, but I'm certainly not going to tell that to my future passengers, especially if it's someone I might want to hang out with and drive around, maybe to Tagaytay, because I know it will freak them out. Heck, I'll admit it, owning this Ford Escape freaks *me* out—and it's only been four days—so much so that while I love this car, I'm ready to convince my dad to sell it and maybe find something else. I'm sure we can clear a profit of at least a hundred thousand pesos on the deal if we move fast. My dad and I can split that up and maybe I can buy an iPhone 4S with my share. It won't be a car though it'll look good too. But first I have to get some papers from the widow. I didn't realize all the IDs and powers of attorney—which apparently she'd managed to get the professor to execute for this and that emergency, in happier days—that you need to transfer a certificate of registration. I'm going back to the wake tomorrow for those odd details, and to listen to all those speeches long-faced people make about what a nice man and brilliant colleague the dear departed was, but also to ask a few more questions of Lalaine Sanvictores. I hate these tired clichés, but there's more to this woman—let's just say there's more to woman—than meets the eye.

CARIÑO BRUTAL

BY R. ZAMORA LINMARK

Tondo

Friday, September 20, 1974, 7:45 a.m.

Lala makes the sign of the cross when she comes upon the naked, mutilated body of Vanessa Blanca hanging from the ancient balete tree on Moriones Street, a block away from the Tutuban train station. Like most of the Tondo residents in the crowd, Lala believes that the tree—beside the small bridge overlooking the shanties along the black, stagnant waters of Canal de la Reina—is haunted by evil spirits. Lala's mother once told her that during the war, the Japs hung a handsome American corporal and his Filipino spy from its branches. She tries to look away, shifting her stare from the grotto of the Virgin Mary that the priests from Santo Niño Church had built inside the hollowed base of the tree. But her gaze keeps returning to the body of the former Miss Gay Tondo Universe.

Vanessa. Vanessa Blanca. Nobody's mistress. Everybody's whore. Last known residence: Olongapo, before she escaped to Tondo after President Marcos declared martial law on September 21, 1972. "Operation Biniboy" had gone into effect, banning transvestites in Olongapo and every other town occupied by the US military.

Vanessa was a *bakla* who preferred sex with straight men. *Bakla. Biniboy. Businessgirl. A puta con huevos.* Add these names up in whatever language and they equal "Beauty." A beauty now reduced to a castrated goddess. Vanessa's long, ash-blond tresses have been shaved off. Her bra and torn panties stuffed in her mouth. The cord of her hip pads, drooping over her back like a cape, is coiled around her neck. Slash marks and stab wounds on her torso. Cigarette burns on her inner thighs. Her penis, severed.

Fourteen-year-old Lala wants to cry but can't. Questions gnaw at her like the balete's aerial roots that, upon touching the earth, will creep toward the tree and feast on what's left of its origin.

Who did this to Vanessa? And why?

Vanessa was her *among ina*. A surrogate mother who made Lala feel and think that she mattered. Who convinced Lala she had a future outside of Tondo, outside of a life that reeked of gang wars at Pier 2, Barrio Matae's shit, and Balut's burning trash.

For three years, Lala lived with Vanessa, learned from her, waited on her. She ran Vanessa's errands, bought her gin and cigarettes, cleaned up after her, massaged her feet. It was Vanessa who gave Lala, born Efren Cruz, her name: Lala L'amour.

Lala did not mind being an *alalay* to Vanessa. Apprenticeship with a renowned Tondo Beauty was coveted by any boy who dreamt of being crowned the next Miss Milky Way, Miss Independence Gay, Muse of the Night, or Miss Gaygaylangin.

In exchange for Lala's loyalty and servitude, Vanessa fed her, dressed her up in the latest creations by Manila's fashion czar, Caloy Badidoy. Vanessa sent Lala to school. First, at Magat Salamat Elementary School, where she finished third in her class. Then, to Gregorio Perfecto High School, where Lala was an honors student until she dropped out five months ago.

When Lala turned twelve, Vanessa started her on the high-end birth control pill "Diane" so Lala could grow breasts. In no time, she blossomed into a young Vanessa. Adopting Vanessa's sexy and sophisticated ways. Accentuating the "A" in attitude,

Vanessa-style. Accepting her Vanessa-given duties as a prelude to beauty with danger.

As for love—Lala had to learn about it the hard way. One day, she came home from school with bruises and a swollen lip because the boy she had a crush on had punched her in the face and called her *Bakla!* When Lala told the story to Vanessa, Vanessa just laughed. "Good for you, Lala. Now, you know better." A week went by and another beating occurred—same bully. Vanessa called Lala "pathetic" and told her to toughen up or else go back to her rat-infested shanty on Pilapil Street and become a washerwoman like her mother.

Vanessa.

Cruel, *cariño brutal* Vanessa. Who believed there was no greater love.

Lala remembers how Vanessa suddenly left one night without saying goodbye to anyone. Not to her pimp Divina Balenciaga from Kambal Krus. Nor to Lola Brigida, the walking drugstore of Pritil, who supplied Vanessa with Madrax, Tussonex cough syrup, Magadol, and the horse tranquilizer fondly known as "Pinoy Ekis."

After weeks without hearing from Vanessa, Lala and the Tondo Beauties wondered if she'd been taken to the dungeons of Camp Crame. Or nabbed by the cops at Precinct Five for violating curfew, raped for alleged theft, and, just for fun, killed. Or maybe she was happily holed up at the Manila Hotel with some American or Japanese businessman.

Lala continues to stare at Vanessa, barely recognizable. Vanessa's ankle catches Lala's eye. *BNG.* Lala doesn't remember Vanessa having a tattoo or getting involved with the Bahala Na Gang, or any gangs for that matter. Vanessa would've told Lala. Besides, Vanessa was not the type to be claimed. A tattoo could only mean she'd spent time in jail where she'd had to choose which gang would protect her—Sigue Sigue Sputnik, Low-Waist, OXO, Commando, Bahala Na. All in exchange for sex.

Lala searches the crowd. She spots Divina Balenciaga comforting Lola Brigita. She is about to wave to Divina when the cops show up.

The crowd—mostly students from Gregorio Perfecto High, street vendors, and market-goers en route to the nearby Divisoria, Manila's mercantile mecca—disperses. Except for a barefooted boy ordered by one of the cops to stay behind.

Lala crosses the street and stands in front of Distelleria Tondeña, a factory that makes the nasty Chinese red wine known as *shoktong*. Fortune-tellers in front of Quiapo Church sell it to rich girls who want to induce miscarriage. The cop hands the kid a knife and gestures to Vanessa's hanging body. Then he walks toward Lala.

"*Ang init,*" the cop says. Removing his cap and wiping the sweat off his forehead with the back of his hand, he asks Lala if she likes the heat. Without waiting for her response, he adds, "*Grabe.* And the day's just beginning."

Cool ka lang, Lala tells herself. Act normal.

Lala keeps her eyes on the boy climbing the balete tree.

"*Sayang si* Vanessa, *no? Ang ganda pa naman niya,*" the cop says, shaking his head and clucking his tongue. *Too bad about Vanessa. She's so beautiful.*

Lala eye-trails the boy now crawling across the lowest branch where Vanessa hangs.

"*Amoy dalaga.*" The cop smiles. *Smells like a virgin.*

The boy cuts the rope with the knife. The rope snaps. Vanessa's body falls.

Lala closes her eyes.

The cop asks Lala if she knows Vanessa.

Lala nods.

"*Close ba kayo?*" the cop asks.

Lala shakes her head no, adding for emphasis, "*Hindi.*" She tells the cop they were neighbors, that her mother did Vanessa's laundry.

The cop then tells Lala to go home before she gets implicated. "*Baka mapahamak ka pa,*" he says, his voice almost sincere.

Lala turns to get a real glimpse of the cop. She notices the jagged scar on his right cheek, his bloodshot deep-set eyes and trimmed mustache. He's handsome, Lala thinks. *Parang action star.* Embroidered on his shirt pocket, in red, is his name. *Eli Cortez.*

Lala walks away. Eli. Eli Cortez. Was he one of the cops infatuated with Vanessa?

Lala looks back and sees that the cop hasn't moved. He nods at her. She takes a deep breath. Relax *ka lang*, she tells herself. He starts walking in her direction. She turns onto Elena Street. At Gregorio Perfecto High School, she begins to slow down. He whistles "Seasons in the Sun." She makes a left on Ricaforte. He catches up to her in front of Iglesia Ni Kristo on Juan Luna Street. They're practically walking side by side on Pavia with its fruit and vegetable stands and milling crowd. She loses him there.

Maybe he's gone back to deal with Vanessa's body, Lala tells herself, back to that tree that is forever growing and rotting.

She enters Liberty Bakery and buys three pieces of *pan de sal*. As she exits, she spots him, Eli, across the street, in front of El Tondeño, which sells embroidered velvet slippers. Eli stands there, waiting. She takes a bite of her bread. Learn from the dead, she tells herself, and walks toward him.

THE UNINTENDED
BY GINA APOSTOL
Ali Mall, Cubao

1. THE STORY SHE WISHES TO TELL

The story Magsalin wishes to tell is about disappearance. Not necessarily about writers who have slipped from this realm, their ideas in melancholy arrest, their notebooks tidy; later one might see the analogy, or at least the pathos of inadequate homage, if one likes symbols. Of course, the story will involve several layers of meaning. There will be a whiff of murder, or maybe a kidnapping, but the clues will be too fraught with personal despair to bear tight scrutiny. Her protagonist is a moviemaker whose scandalous father precedes her fame. Her name has an Italian flavor, Chiara or Lucia, with the first C glottal and the latter *c* a florid *ch*: she is Kiarrrra, or Luchiiiia—Magsalin has yet to decide. Both names mean *clear*, or *lucidity*, or something that has to do with *light*, something vaguely linked to *eyesight*, hence to *knowing*, thence to paradox. It is Chiara/Lucia's body that may go missing.

2. A MYSTERIOUS E-MAIL MESSAGE

The subject line intrigues her: *Translator needed, meet me at Muhammad Ali Mall.* The message must be from a foreigner. No one calls the mall by that name. Some Filipinos do not even know the seedy building is named for the greatest, Muhammad Ali.

She has just arrived from New York, on vacation in her birthplace, Manila, to continue a task that she believes has great spiritual potential, though the rewards are yet to surface. She is beginning a mystery novel.

The curtness of the subject line, Magsalin thinks, is rude. She thinks the message is a joke, a hoax drummed up by her writer friends, a bunch of alcoholics hiding out, often in pork-induced stupor, in Flushing, Queens. Magsalin ignores the message.

Later, she searches Chiara's name online. She finds an item mentioning her arrival only *18 hours ago,* an innocuous piece with a photo of the filmmaker at Manila International Airport, wearing huge shades and a safari outfit. The report speculates she is *scouting sites for a movie.* No quote emerges from the director herself.

Magsalin checks Chiara's cred through praxino.com, Magsalin's website of choice for occasional curiosities. A tour operator reports that Tom Cruise was sighted in March in the Ilocos, sporting an ugly ingrown toenail revealed by beach flip-flops. She learns that Sandra Bullock did not buy her black baby in the area near the old US air force base in Pampanga. Madonna's orphanage in Malawi is hemorrhaging millions, bilked by savvy entrepreneurs. Eric Clapton's late son's former nanny, a Chavacano, remains in seclusion in Zamboanga, still mourning her single lapse. Donatella Versace did not slap her maid. Finally, she turns up a video of Chiara Brasi, a wan and wavering figure, in one of those canned interviews to promote a project. This video is also quoted in FabSugar, the *Emory Wheel, Irish Times,* Moviefone: Chiara rode a helicopter over Manila with her father, the war movie director. A fond memory, in 1976. Someone had unhinged the helicopter's doors, and she looks out as if the sky is her vestibule.

Magsalin goes back to the e-mail, composes a response. She hits send.

* * *

3. MEETING AT A PASTRY SHOP

During the best of times Ali Mall is a decrepit, cramped cement block of shops hosting Rugby glue sniffers, high school truants, and depressed carnival men on break. It was built in 1976, a paean to the Thrilla in Manila, which took place directly across the street at the Araneta Coliseum in Cubao, site of the match that destroyed the career of the heavyweight champion of the world, Joe "The Gorilla" Frazier, and the source of our modern discomfort perhaps—a sense of the futility of earthly striving—whenever one thinks about Muhammad Ali. Cubao is the omen of Ali's shambling shadow. Cubao heralds an incommunicable fall.

Even at noon Ali Mall is creepy. The circus is nearby, and a creaky carousel winds around like some tiresome concept of eternity. Magsalin enters by the basement annex, through the Philippine Airlines office toward the Botak shop and a trinket store selling Hello Kitty barrettes. A security guard is texting by some plywood boards, next to an idling clown. Magsalin heads straight to a bakery selling cinnamon buns and *pan de sal*.

She notes, like a skillful detective, that her likely client, wearing a tank top, panama hat, and tan wedges, is attempting the incognito look. But the designer shoes (Clergerie) and in-congruous shades (also French: Chanel) are amateurish. Even an idiot would know she's rich. Magsalin has not lived twelve years in New York for nothing. This woman at the counter, drinking bottled water and not eating her bread, has the luxury of looking underdressed, no-nonsense. She's flat-chested. She shows Magsalin a thick manila envelope, bulging with papers. A manuscript.

Chiara is muckle-mouthed. Her charm is furtive: now you see it, now it seems only dreamed. She is shy. That is what Mag-salin thinks, until she recognizes that the faraway gaze (obvious even behind Chanel), the averted angle of her chin, the awk-ward pose on the stool, the surprisingly uninteresting monotone are in fact indifference. Magsalin considers leaving. How dare this stranger look so self-assured? But then, Magsalin thinks, the woman also looks sedated, drugged.

But really, how is Magsalin to know? Her own buzz of choice is cheap Chilean pinot noir, hardly a peril.

Anyhow, Chiara's past is full of shady anecdotes. At least, her father's is—and the newspapers used to be full of Luca Brasi's es-capades. It was in Lubao, Pampanga, that he had an affair with both a costume designer and an electrician during the filming of his Vietnam War movie, now more or less forgotten—though at one point it was thought *The Unintended* would challenge the genius of Francis Ford Coppola's *Apocalypse Now*, except be less commercial. He and Coppola are practically contemporaries; both grew up in New York. But while the one has a genial pater-nal aura, even in the documentary by his faintly bitter, long-suf-fering wife, the other is satyric, greasy, saturnine, and unstable.

It is no wonder that his daughter has the off-putting tem-perament of someone only intermittently aware.

4. CHIARA'S TRIP

Chiara affirms she is the daughter of the director of *The Un-intended*. Magsalin confesses she saw the film several times in her teens. She recalls watching it frame by frame in a muggy class along Katipunan, called "Locations/Dislocations," about the phantasmal voids in Vietnam War movies shot in equally blighted areas that are not in fact Vietnam. Within the disturb-ing web of contorted allusions, hidden historiographic anxiety, political ironies, and astounding art direction resident in a single frame, for instance, of a fissured bridge—in real life dynamited by the Japanese in 1943 and still unrepaired in 1976, and rebuilt specifically and reexploded spectacularly in a filmic faux-napalm scene against a mystic pristine river actually already polluted by local dynamite fishers—the movie kept putting Magsalin to sleep, for whatever reason, though she omits that detail before the filmmaker's daughter. There was something both engrossing and pathetic about it, about reconstructing the trauma of whole countries through a film's illusive palimpsest, and what was most disturbing, of course, was that, on one level, the professor's point was undeniably true: our identities are irremediably mediated—but that does not mean Magsalin has to keep thinking about it.

Chiara seems unconcerned, however, by the scholarly implications of her father's cult classic; at least she seems unburdened. She nods absently at Magsalin's furrowed approximations of her memory, as if she, Chiara, has heard it all before, as if she needs another Adderall. What she really needs, Chiara says, almost upsetting Magsalin's cup of chai, is someone to accompany her on a trip.

"Where to?" asks Magsalin.

"I need to get to Samar."

5. WHY SAMAR??!!

Chiara has vague but pleasant memories of the times she spent with her father in the tropics. Specifically, she was in Quezon City and in Angeles, Pampanga, but she would learn that only later, online. She was four in 1975. She remembers a skating rink, being crowned Miss Philippines in games with tiny beauty-contest-obsessed girls who always let her win, and getting lice from goats owned by a visiting tribe of mountain people.

Chiara has a fractured memory of one night in Manila during the city's seasonal rains. Her mother, usually all nerves, a Ukrainian Jew brought up on stories of pogroms, who turned to Christian Science then hatha yoga after the divorce, is agitated, sitting down and getting back up to protect a flickering flame. Oddly, the Philippines drove her mother's persecution complex underground, and she lives in almost Buddhist calm amid the lizards on the ceilings, monstrous cockroaches in the toilet, sewer animals in the garden, and nubile prostitutes promenading all around the seedy American military bases. This is significant, as Chiara's mother is, quite frankly, a millionaire. Her mother is spoiled and used to getting her way. She had given her husband his Hollywood start. But it is as if the desperate indignities of living in a perpetually fallen state, among lives she shares and witnesses with a perplexed gaze, has lent Chiara's mother peace, a converse calm, that she has not regained since.

Perhaps this explains Chiara's sense at times that a vulnerable world could be an oasis.

The shadows of her mother's single candle and the sounds of a gecko on the wall are the night's only cartographic points. Otherwise, she and her mother and her father are suspended, the only people in a universal void, rocking in a gigantic cradle hanging above Manila's awful monsoon winds. Chiara is happy. Chiara is lying with her curly four-year-old head on her huge, sweating father's lap. The famously methodical director is picking lice, one pinch following another, a rich rhythmic tug mauling her tender scalp, each tug pleasingly soporific, a victorious bloodbath on her father's hands. She doesn't remember her father cursing every time he finds a pest and crushing it with his purple thumb, though her mother has pointed out those gross details. It is the most pleasing memory of her childhood, that blackout night, her father picking out lice from her hair until she falls asleep: it is pleasing to recall her dad, busy with formidable things, determined to rid her of all the bugs he can find, to use his director powers to seek out her vermin, to squash the blood out from the pests' abominable veins, as if he is crushing the concentrated frustration arising from the calamities of his unsteady enterprise, the making of his cursed monumental film.

Chiara was Googling idly, with nothing on her mind, in her mother's mansion. Then she went Oedipal. She Googled her father's film, *The Unintended*, and the year production began: 1975. She never thought she would find an item of interest, nothing memorable, not even an inch of a pitch for a horror script or a jotting for her sundry journal. But on pages twenty-four through thirty in the search results, she started clicking. Muhammad Ali's historic match against Joe Frazier on October 1, 1975. Miss Universe Amparo Muñoz has become a soft-porn star and is stripped of her crown. The bells of Balangiga, some religious items stolen from a Philippine island, remain missing. The first multilevel shopping mall in the Philippines rises in tribute to Muhammad Ali's victory. Another article on the ambush in Balangiga of American soldiers of the 9th US Infantry Regiment on an island called Samar in 1901. What the heck was going on?

Online, an unrelated catastrophe was ambushing her father's film. Balangiga, Samar, kept coming up, neck and neck with Muhammad Ali.

6. An Alternate Story

It turns out a Filipino scholar has written a paper linking the massacre of civilians in Balangiga, Samar, 1901, to the 1968 Vietnam massacre that frames her father's unfortunate film. As some viewers might recall, *The Unintended* is a story about a teenage kid, Tommy O'Connell, who fails to be court-martialed for acts he has committed in a hamlet, code-named Pinkville, that he, along with his fellow men of Charlie Company, razes to the ground. Tommy tells his story so the world does not forget the horror of his experience.

The Balangiga incident of 1901, on the other hand, is a true story in two parts, a blip in the Philippine-American War (itself a blip in the Spanish-American War, which is a blip in outbreaks of imperial hysteria in Southeast Asian wars, which are blips in the infinite cycle of human aggression in the dying days of this dying planet, et al.). Part one: an uprising of Filipino rebels against the American outpost (the exposition here would be a fascinating movie in its own right, though with too many color-ful local details) leads to the deaths of thirty-six Americans, with twenty-two wounded and four missing in action. Part two: The US commanding general demands in retaliation the murder of every Filipino in Samar above ten years of age, and blood bathes the province. Americans savage—"kill and burn" is the techni-cal term—close to three thousand Filipinos, men, women, and children, in a vengeful massacre of such proportions that the subsequent court-martial of the general, Jacob H. "Howling Wil-derness" Smith, causes a sensation in the American press when the events become public in 1902.

A noted scholar, Professor Estrella Espejo, points out on-line that the Samar incident also implicates a Charlie Company (though it was of the wrong regiment, the 11th Infantry, not the 20th or the 23rd Division). As in Vietnam, only one or two American officers are tried for the Philippine affair. The 1901 court-martialed counterpart of the Vietnam War's Colonel Cal-ley (a shadowy figure in her father's movie, unnamed for legal reasons) is the infamous General Jacob Smith, who ordered the Filipino deaths by making memorable staccato statements: "I want no prisoners. I wish you to kill and burn. The more you kill and burn, the better it will please me." There is also the general's resonant phrase, which made his name: "The interior of Samar must be made a howling wilderness." According to Professor Es-pejo, the repulsive yet fascinating Smitty Jakes, the Kilgore-like lieutenant whose pathological patriotism is the most troubling yet truest aspect of Luca Brasi's film, is a nod to the butcher of Balangiga. Lastly, the movie's hero, the guilt-ridden wraith, Tommy O'Connell, Espejo says, as if resting her case, is clearly the West Point–educated commanding officer of the Samar outpost, twenty-six-year-old Captain Thomas W. Connell, a moralist whose meager ethics measured in full the absurdity of the American cause.

7. Translations

Magsalin does not know what to make of Chiara's globe-trotting story. For one thing, it is past one o'clock, and outside the truant boys are shrugging back into their white polo shirts, the uniform of all the Catholic schools that dot EDSA, done with their lunch-hour video games, and the circus men are winding their way out of the mall like blind mice, every clown in deep-black Ray-Ban knockoffs, wiping off rice grains and chorizo oil from their greasepaint lips, and still Magsalin does not get exactly why Chiara is globe-trotting.

What puts Magsalin off at the pastry shop is Chiara's voice. It is nasal. Her monotone does not help, a bored flatness, even in the most interesting parts, that keeps Magsalin, or the pastry shop waitress, or anyone else willing to listen amid the humid baking scones and moist *pan de sal*, at bay, as if an invisible wall, maybe socioeconomic, exists between Chiara's indifference and Magsalin's attention.

Magsalin's taxable occupation is to translate, hence her professional name: Magsalin. (It means *to translate* in her maternal grandfather's tongue, Tagalog.) Perhaps the envelope Chiara has offered Magsalin contains the rough draft of the script that Chiara wrote on a lethargic April afternoon in a mansion in the New York mountains. Maybe Chiara's next project is an art house political film, á la Costa-Gavras's Z, to be shot on location in the actual country in which the plot occurs, a film of dizzying unheard-of realism, hence the need for translations into the actual language of the hapless citizens in the process of being killed by the occupation forces. Who knows?

Magsalin is aware of those scenes in Hollywood movies when, requiring an actor to speak a conveniently alien tongue, the character starts speaking an inappropriate one, like Tagalog. The prayer of the Javanese man in *The Year of Living Dangerously*. The possessed sibyl cursing out Keanu Reeves in *Constantine*. And, of course, the amusing scene of the nasty, tiny Ewoks in *Star Wars: Return of the Jedi*.

In the trade there are technical names for these short-term projects.

Inversions provide a set of unmatched signifiers that, if understood, does not require logical coherence. This is the case of the Bahasa-Indonesian prayer in Peter Weir's movie. The Indonesian prays the Our Father in Tagalog, not Bahasa—that is, he need not be coherent; it's the concept that counts. *Inversions* are opposed to *obversions*—that is, providing a set of unmatched signifiers that, if understood, are generally insulting. The naughty Ewok dialogue in the *Star Wars* film, a set of pungent Tagalog epigrams, is, of course, a basic Filipino fuck you to the universe. What Magsalin expects is that Chiara's script will require *reversions*: a set of matching signifiers that, if reversed, will portray the privileged language as in fact the other, and vice versa. *Perversions*, of course, produce scant good. Lastly, *conversions*, the most difficult of these types of translations, Magsalin simply refuses to attempt.

What interests Magsalin about Chiara is not the prospect of a job but her likely disappearance. In Magsalin's mystery novel, Chiara will leave Ali Mall by a wrong turn, through the plywood board tunnel, a sign announcing the mall owner's promise of a *NEW ALI MALL! COMING SOON!* put up ten years ago. The security guard, shutting off his cell phone, will give Chiara clear directions in English, but she will not understand his accent. Chiara has a sense of being lost amid the warped plywood, the tunnel is so spooky and haphazard it has the impression of not even being lit, though makeshift electrical wires become obvious when her vision adjusts. The tunnel spills into the harsh light of the fluorescent bulbs of the decaying merry-go-round outside, where tricycle drivers waiting for clients pick their teeth on ill-painted horses. Magsalin knows the area well from her days as a serial bookworm at Alemar's and National Bookstore, in the years 1976–1980, when she went to school nearby. It occurs to her that the details she has evoked in the last few sentences might bear traces of her memory's obsolescence, and Chiara's plaintive future, therefore, her kidnapping by a pair of muscular, Ray-Ban-wearing goons (of course, they are dressed as clowns) is set among details of an obsolete past.

Chiara's struggle will be unseen, though one might expect a stray schoolboy to be lighting a match nearby, polo shirt half on (he's a bit malnourished); but the irony is that the boy, smoking his last forbidden cigarette before he's expected in gym class, will be looking at the comic book he has just bought with carefully saved change. He is in no state to observe a famous film director being shoved into a waiting tricycle, an ordinary passenger pedi-cab painted in the usual deranged Manila hues.

Magsalin, on the other hand, will be wandering Ali Mall. Done with the exhausting interview with the filmmaker, and feeling a bit nauseous, still unsure what has brought her here, not just to Cubao but to her country, Magsalin clutches the thick manila envelope and travels Ali Mall in a daze. The mall is now quite modern, practically Singaporean; at the same time, the familiarity is distracting. There is a schizoid confabulation between the new upscale fixtures, such as the gleaming escalators and neon in the food court, which now looks like a strip club, and the ratty hair-accessories wrapped in dusty plastic that seem to have been in the Cardam chain of shoe shops since they opened in 1976. What is true perhaps is that, after the vertigo of listening to the story of Chiara Brasi, Magsalin feels unreal, and the world has an illusory aspect, part memory, part script, the split state of a spectator providing her own unpaid translations in a movie in which she exists.

8. CHIARA'S MOVIE

That is the effect Chiara wants for her next movie, she says. It will have an emptiness at its heart: a war movie not unlike her father's, but without its coherence. A secret will lie in its structure, like a dumb grenade. It will be set in 1901, the inverse of '68, but no one will be the wiser. Anachronisms, false starts, scarlet clues, a noirish insistence on the pathetic pursuit of human truths will pervade its miserable (quite thin) plot, and while the mystery will not unravel, to a select few it will provide the satisfaction of an unfathomable rage.

This is the part when, to Magsalin, as Chiara tells her story, the filmmaker drops her guard. Chiara gains a hint of, let's say, *embodiment*, losing that slightly offensive appearance of tactful sedation. She becomes animated, finally munching on the proffered *pan de sal*, buttering it up on all sides, crust and filling both, and her straight blond hair is getting caught in her gleaming, jutting, expensively symmetrical upper teeth.

She explains why a visit to Samar is necessary. A spiritual journey.

"You know that is not a normal thing to say about Samar," Magsalin says.

Chiara ignores her.

She had a conversion online, she says. She had a conversion into the world of the Filipino rebels of 1901. It was as if, she explains to Magsalin, she had entered a portal and become the body of a Filipino farmer disguised as a devout Catholic woman carrying a machete inside his billowing peasant skirt, hoping to kill a GI.

"You were hallucinating," Magsalin replies. "Do you know what was really in your mother's heirloom apple compote in the Catskills? What were you drinking?"

Professor Estrella Espejo's papers on Balangiga, *The Unintended: A Consequence*, Parts 1, 3, and 6, were on kirjasto, a WordPress blog by the same tenure-track associate professor in San Diego, and a remote server that, when clicked upon, apologized for the inconvenience but due to copyright questions, et cetera . . . Chiara's efforts to find the scholar's contacts were fruitless, until she located an exchange in a comments section on inq7.net involving Espejo and Magsalin.

"Wait a minute," Magsalin demands. "When was this?"

Chiara takes out a notebook from her huge Hermés bag.

"August 15, 2000. You likened the *bitter, essentializing determinist* Professor Espejo to the coyote in the cartoon about the Road Runner, saying, quote, *like Wile E. Coyote you keep setting your traps though it is only you who bites,* unquote."

"That was in reference to her loony-tunes theory that Juan Luna, the Filipino painter, must be Jack the Ripper, because Luna was also in Europe at the time of the Ripper. You see, Juan Luna had killed his wife. She thinks that the death of Paz Chiching Luna is the last Ripper death. Estrella is insane."

"You had another run-in with her in 2004."

"She gets these history-worms in her head and won't let go."

"It was about my father's film."

"Yeah, yeah."

"You read closely the scene in which Tommy O'Connell shoots a woman and her daughter hiding something in a rickshaw."

"They were hiding a book."

"It was a diary. You noted that the camera panned over a few quick words, meant to be in French."

"It was supposed to be the diary of the woman's dead husband, a murdered rebel. A list of his descriptions, his trifling observations of his kid, the girl Tommy has just killed—and the now-dead mother had only been trying to keep his personal possessions intact. But on screen, the actual words, if you stopped the frame, were in Waray, the language of Samar."

"Your idea was that the sentences in my dad's film were actual pages from a diary of a rebel soldier from the Philippine-American War."

"I imagined your dad was alluding to the other war and making a connection. I wondered then why the Philippine diary, a red herring in his text, was so repressed. Why was it that in his press conferences your dad made no references to the 1901 incident at all? I mean, as I said, look at the names in his movie: Smitty Jakes, Tommy O'Connell. Read *The Ordeal of Samar* and you have your dad's movie right there."

"I did."

"Read *The Ordeal of Samar*?"

"I got the Joseph Schott book, yes. It was disturbing, but not in ways that could make a good movie."

"So you cheated. You went off the Internet and read an actual book."

Chiara laughs. Then she says: "So I want to know. Are you Professor Estrella Espejo?"

Magsalin almost topples off the stool. She starts coughing, stuff is coming out of her nose, and the waitress offers her water and a napkin.

Magsalin takes a long sip. "Hell no," she says, putting down the glass. "I wouldn't be caught dead being Estrella Espejo. She's a lunatic with astasia-abasia tied up in IV tubes on an island off the South China Sea. I mean, the North Philippine Sea, depending on your disposition."

She stares at the filmmaker, daring her to contradict.

"Yeah, I know," says Chiara. "Estrella Espejo is something else. She told me to get in touch with you if I wanted to go to Balangiga. She said she could not help me, because she's in the hospital and unstable."

"You can say that again. Did she give you my e-mail?"

"And fax."

"She's a shit."

"Pardon?"

"She makes things up and won't let go. Take the details of your father's film. First, Charlie Company: every third goddamned company is called Charlie. Anyone who took Citizen's Army Training, as Espejo did since she lived under Marcos's martial law, knows that. Second, Smitty Jakes, Jacob Smith. Okay, sounds alike. Tommy O'Connell, Thomas Connell. Sounds convincing. Clearly one text is lifted from another. She goes on making a case about names. The point is not the coincidence of the names, or their intentional equivalence. The one-to-one correspondence between history and fiction is not interesting. It's a logical fallacy to mistake the parallel with the teleological—it's not clear that God exists between parallel lines. I mean, if you are going to steal my idea, at least make something useful out of it. The question, it seems to me, is how to keep the incident from recurring. I mean, what the fuck is the point of knowing history's loops if we remain its bloody victims?"

"Do you think there are parallel universes and we are stuck in the one made up only of bad movie plots?"

"I think we are stuck in the bad movie plots we make ourselves."

"I think we are stuck in someone's movie."

"What do you mean?"

Magsalin looks hard through Chiara Brasi's shades. Chiara does not take them off even when she accidentally gets butter on them from the cinnamon buns. Now that Chiara has already buttered the *pan de sal*, she starts buttering the cinnamon buns, which are already buttered. Magsalin does not detect irony in her monotone.

"You know that is only margarine," Magsalin says. "It just looks like butter."

Chiara ignores her.

Chiara lectures, moving her slim hands in geometric patterns, enunciating her vowels, at some points cocking her head to one side as if she is looking for the right word, her wide mouth pouted upward as she brushes her sleek hair off her shoulder, revealing her lack of cleavage. Magsalin once saw her on *Inside the Actors Studio* and feels the need to reach for an index card in case the filmmaker expects her to ask Big Questions.

"I think we are stuck in someone's movie, and the director is still laying out his scraps of script, trying to figure out his ending. He does not have an ending. Everything around him has the possibility of becoming part of his mystery plot—his lost love for his wife, that fly over there licking the sugar on the bun, the clown in the corner playing with a knife, a moment in a mirror store in New York when he sees himself replicated through his camera lens in all the mirrors except he cannot see his eyes, the unanswered questions about a writer's death, the unanswered questions about a country's war, that schoolboy carefully folding a white shirt and tucking it neatly into a paper bag, a heart attack he has in 1977 when his movie is still not done, when it has a beginning and an ending but no idea, and twelve hundred feet of unedited stock, with takes, retakes, and other duplications. That is what we are: twelve hundred feet of unedited stock, doing things over and over, and we are waiting for the cut. But who is the director? What is our wait for? I would like to make a movie in which the spectator understands that she is in a work of someone else's construction and yet as she watches she is devising her own translations for the movie in which she in fact exists. What is convenient about Balangiga is that it seems as if *The Unintended* was constructed out of the story of Samar's parts, but it is also true that it's the other way around. My father's movie also produces, for us, the tale of Balangiga. This goes without saying. One story told may unbury another, and all the dead are resurrected. Recurrence is only an issue of not knowing how the film should end."

Magsalin takes an index card and reads aloud the first Big Question: "But is it about knowing how a film should end, or not knowing its shape?"

"A film has no shape if it does not know its end."

Magsalin takes an index card and reads aloud the second Big Question: "But is it about knowing how a film should end, or the fact that it has no end, or its end is multiple, like desire's prongs?"

"Touché."

Magsalin takes an index card and reads aloud the third Big Question: "Do you know that a clown is going to kidnap you?"

"In a mystery, clowns are always significant."

Magsalin takes an index card and reads aloud the last Big Question: "What is in the manila envelope?"

"If you take it, you will see."

9. The Thrilla in Manila

"Okay," says Magsalin, taking the envelope. "I'll see what I can do about Samar. I know a few people who can help you."

"Thank you," Chiara says in that annoying nasal monotone.
"How do you get out of here?"

"Just follow the signs. There are detours for the exits. They're
renovating, you know."

"Are you leaving too?"

Magsalin thinks she will take her up on it, on the forlorn
implication in Chiara's little-girl voice that she would like some
company, that she is scared of Cubao and her impulsive clueless
spiritual adventure, which only people as rich or thoughtless as
Chiara can suddenly get in their heads and then stupidly follow
through; and yes, Magsalin will lead her to the exit and get her
safely to her hotel.

"I want to take a spin around the mall," Magsalin says. "I'll
hang around here a bit. I'll see you later."

The waitress offers the check. Chiara hands over a credit
card. The waitress shakes her head. Magsalin takes out her non-
Hermés bag and pays with cash.

"Thanks," Chiara says.

"No problem."

"My father saw that fight, you know. Ringside."

"Ali-Frazier?"

"Yeah. The Thrilla in Manila. We lived nearby in—let's see,
it's in my notebook. Greenhills."

"That's in Pasig, not Quezon City."

"Oh. The Internet was wrong."

"Figures."

"The Thrilla in Manila," Chiara repeats, and then she gets
up, just like that, leaving Magsalin and the *pan de sal* shop.

Bitch.

Chiara is in the dark hallway, and Magsalin has to follow
behind. The filmmaker is blocking Magsalin's exit and gazing,

as if mentally noting its pros and cons as a film location, at the boarded-up spaces beyond Philippine Airlines, the scaffolding that might be a promised escalator or a remnant of someone's change of mind.

"Muhammad Ali Mall. What an interesting tribute."

"Ali Mall," Magsalin corrects, wondering if Chiara will ever budge from the door. "Yeah, it's dumb."

"Dumpy." Chiara turns, smiling but not moving. "But not dumb. It's sweet. I like tributes. I've read all the books about that fight, you know. I guess because I see it through the lens of my childhood. After my father finished *The Unintended*, you know, after Manila, my parents divorced. I lived with my mom. The last time we were together was in Manila. The Thrilla in Manila. I've watched that match over and over again. On DVD. Round 6. When Ali says to Frazier—"

"They tol' me Joe Frazier was all washed up!"

"And Frazier goes—"

"They lied, champ—they lied!"

"Hah!" Chiara claps her hands. "You do a mean Frazier."

"Thank you. Were you for Ali or Frazier?" Magsalin asks.

"I love Muhammad Ali."

"Do you think he's real?"

"More real than I," says Chiara. "He's the Greatest."

Just for that, Magsalin thinks, she'll do whatever this spoiled brat says.

"Myself, I liked Frazier," says Magsalin.

"Really? But why?"

"Because he wasn't actually an ugly motherfucker. He was no gorilla. Except Ali, the director, made him up."

A motif of the renovated Ali Mall is a series of commissioned portraits of the boxer framed in glass at strategic points, like altars. The reflexive signifiers, most of them tacky, are not tongue-in-cheek. They are serious gestures of veneration. One has a wilted flower on its ledge, as if left by an admirer (candy wrappers and cigarette stubs also decorate the shrine). While the corporate intention of co-opting the Greatest in order to shill shoes is obvious, the beauty of the intertextual display—the portraits that modify the mall, and the mall that is an appositive of the portraits—is that presence confounds purpose. The portraits do make Ali as absurd as the corporation promoting meaning from dubious intentions. Passing them by her first time in amusement, at another in alarm, at several outright laughing, Magsalin spends the afternoon searching the mall for all the images. One, a giant reproduction like an advertisement, is done in painstaking flatness. Ali's nose is as big as the letter A in the word *CHAMPION*. It has graffiti all over its wall. But when you look close, expecting obscenity, instead you find sincere compliments, some of them mistaken: *ali is da greatest! I saw the HBO, THRILLA!, r.i.p. Muhammad Ali, floats like a butterfly, sings like a bee*. At this point, though perhaps in the future it will change, Muhammad Ali is in fact still alive. Oddly, even the errors count. In another, a cubist Ali in a relaxed pose, clearly allusive, looks like Pablo Picasso in an early self-portrait, wearing a white *camisa*. Another illustrates a Filipino pantheon of assorted black idols—Stevie Wonder, Michael Jackson, Kareem Abdul Jabbar, the kid from *Diff'rent Strokes*, Gloria Gaynor of "I Will Survive" fame, and their forefather, Muhammad Ali—descending in order somewhat like Marcel Duchamp's *Nude Descending a Staircase*, but not. To pan on each of these is a slice of time, precious in Chiara's movie, so the viewer does wonder at its meanings, juxtaposed as they are with a scene in Magsalin's story—a kidnapping left hanging.

PART III

THEY LIVE BY NIGHT

OLD MONEY

BY JESSICA HAGEDORN

Forbes Park

OUT OF THE BLUE

P aco texted me, asking for a ride. No explanation, no *hey man I miss u*, no *please*. It had been—according to the dates crossed off on my calendar—exactly five weeks since he'd disappeared. Everyone thought he was dead. I texted Paco right back, like nothing was out of the ordinary: *k cu soon :D*

I couldn't resist signing off with that smiley face. It was the kind of corny crap that got on Paco's nerves.

THE WAIT

Three more days of heavy rain went by. The sewers backed up in certain parts of Manila. No one seemed too concerned. On the fourth day, I got another text from Paco, this time naming a location. Then another one seconds later: *dont b L8.*

His terse, cryptic messages were oddly flattering. Was I—the *balikbayan* son of a dying nobody father—the only one left in Manila he could trust?

FAMILY

About Nicanor, my dying nobody father. Tita Moning had paid his hospital bill and taken him in after the doctors at Philippine General let her know that there was nothing more they could do for him. Pop had nowhere else to go. His young, pregnant Japayuki girlfriend was long gone.

Moning was Pop's sister, a wiz at making money. Her savvy little start-ups had made her a rich woman: Moning's Vulcanizing & Auto Repair, Moning's Washeteria & Dry Clean, Moning's Ang Sarap! Cupcake Café. Like everyone else in my family, I leaned on my aunt whenever I was in trouble. Like when I lost my job and went into rehab and was behind on rent and living on food stamps and getting pretty fucking desperate. My own mother was shacked up with this redneck in Reno and—just like my pop—couldn't be counted on for anything. But Tita Moning came through like she always did. Wire transfer, sympathy, and not too many probing questions.

So when she Skyped to say that I should get my sorry ass out of Long Beach and back to Manila, how could I say no?

I'll pay your airfare. You can stay with us, Junior. My new house has plenty bedrooms. And a swimming pool.

That's nice, Tita Moning.

She let out one of those heavy Filipino sighs. Your father does not have long for this earth.

I know, Tita Moning. I know.

Cancer of the brain, lungs, liver, esophagus—

Got it, Tita Moning. Jeez.

The sharpness of my tone took my aunt by surprise. She looked like she wanted to reach through the laptop screen and smack me good and hard.

After a few seconds of silence, Tita Moning dropped another bomb. She'd gotten me a job.

WHAT?

It's waiting for you, Junior. My *kumadre's* son manages a call center in Pasig.

But I don't know anything about—

So what? You sound American and that's what counts.

* * *

Mabuhay

My cousin Louie met me at the airport the night I arrived. All smiles and hugs, scrutinizing me furtively from head to toe. My no-brand jeans and plain black T-shirt undoubtedly a huge disappointment. We used to be close as kids. But when my mom left my pop and whisked me off to the States without warning, Louie and I lost touch. I was keeping up with him on Facebook, though. Louie called himself a men's fashion blogger and had quite a following, though his blog was nothing more than snapshots of stoned guys in clubs flaunting the latest hipster gear. Last time I checked, Louie had 5,151 Facebook "friends." I was one of them.

The car was a brand-new Lexus, the driver a solemn man named Fausto. He addressed me as "sir" and Louie as "señorito." Instead of having Fausto take us straight to my aunt's house like he was supposed to, Señorito Louie ordered him to make a detour to the Fort.

Wait till you see how Fort Bonifacio's changed, Louie gushed. *Talagang galing!* Then he asked, You still understand Tagalog, Nick?

My Tagalog sucks, but I get the gist.

Up ahead was a glitzy fortress that took up the entire block, pulsing with lights. Louie ordered Fausto to drop us off and find somewhere to park. And don't forget to keep your phone on, Louie said in English.

Fausto nodded. *Oo po, señorito.*

It was already past midnight. Won't your mom be pissed off at us? I remember asking Louie.

She'll blame Fausto, Louie said. Maybe even fire him.

Galing, Ano?

The line of trendsetters snaked around the block. We strolled up to the front of the line, ignoring the resentful stares of everyone around us. The gatekeeper stood by the entrance with a couple of security guys. Louie caught me eyeing the guy's shoes. They were black and silver bowling shoes, really slick.

Prada. I have the same pair in gold, Louie said. *Galing, ano?*

Mr. Prada waved us in.

Last of the Coño Kids

It felt good in there. The delirious mob thrashing around to a thumping soundtrack, desperate to have fun. We grabbed a couple of drinks at the downstairs bar and watched them dance. I wasn't supposed to be drinking, but there you go. Three months of sobriety right out the window. Louie kept making vicious comments about people's haircuts, outfits, fat asses, no-asses, who was definitely hot and who wasn't. It was funny at first, but got old really fast.

And then they walked in. It was really the guy who first caught my attention. Sweeping into the club like he owned it, with those green eyes and a killer smile. A swanlike girl in a tiny dress and high-heeled boots hung onto his arm, like she was afraid she might fall down or something.

Who's *that*? I asked Louie.

He goes by Paco.

And the girl?

Gala.

She a model?

When you can get her to show up, Louie snickered.

I was introduced as Louie's long-lost cousin from California. Paco and Gala were clearly coked up, Paco in an expansive, convivial mood. He invited us to join them upstairs in the cordoned-off VIP lounge. Where he said the service was one on one, the music *different* and not as loud. We slid into a spacious booth in a shadowy corner.

Welcome to my satellite office, Paco said. We all laughed.

Gala complained about the air-con being on too high. Paco gave her his jacket. A waiter scurried over and said drinks were on the house. Paco didn't seem surprised. He told the waiter to bring a bottle of Rémy for the table, without asking us what we wanted. Then he lit a cigarette. I noticed the tattoo of thorns around his wrist.

Q&A

Most of us can't wait to get out of this country and live somewhere else. Why'd you move back here, Nick?

I heard the surfing's awesome.

It is. You a surfer, Nick?

Are *you?*

I'm a businessman. Ready for a toot?

Uh-Oh

I followed him to the men's room like a meek little lamb. We locked ourselves in one of the stalls. Two searing hits of Paco's coke and I lost my inhibition. I leaned in and kissed his mouth. The kiss was gruff and quick. He pushed me away with a smile.

Not so fast, kid.

We went back to the table without saying a word. Louie and Gala were waiting for us.

Can we have some too? Gala cooed.

Beautiful People

Paco dealt out of an apartment in one of those creaky, prewar buildings in Malate that his family owned. He could get you anything, Louie said. Even the latest and most expensive high, which was crack. You're fucking kidding me, I said. Crack?

Louie shrugged. He always insisted I come along with him to score, for some mysterious reason. Misery loves company, I guess. Paco's clientele was small and definitely A-list, with money to burn. Louie—a thirty-year-old brat who depended on his mother's generous monthly allowance and had never worked a day in his life—was one of the lucky few. I knew I was out of my league, and made every effort to stay away. Plus, I couldn't stand Paco acting like I didn't exist. He'd been cold toward me since that night at the club, and had eyes only for Gala. Once I started working at the call center, it got a little easier to stay away. The job sucked, but I actually got off saying shit like: *American Express Customer Service, Ralph speaking. How may I help you?*

Ralph. Steve. Randy. Whatever. I finally made it to an AA meeting held in this sweet little community center close to my aunt's house in Quezon City. But there were too many born-again freaks in the room and I never went back. As the weeks of stifling heat and torrential rains dragged on, I resolved:

1. To stop thinking about Paco.
2. To stop hanging out with Louie.
3. To not get fired.
4. To buy a car.
5. To move out of Tita Moning's and rent my own apartment.
6. To help my father die a dignified death.

Yeah, yeah, yeah.

I did manage to buy a car. A 2005 Corolla from the call center agent who worked in the cubicle next to me. The kind of car that Louie wouldn't be caught dead driving or riding in, which was fine by me.

SPIRAL

One night the craving was so strong, I slipped out of the house and drove to Paco's apartment. The maids were asleep. My aunt and uncle were in Cebu, overseeing the opening of another Ang

Sarap! franchise. Louie was at some mall, covering a men's fashion show for his fucking blog. No one was around to ask where I
was going. My father lay in the downstairs guest room dreaming
his morphine dreams, watched over by the private nurse Tita
Moning had hired. I peered into the room on my way out the
door. His mouth was slack and open. He didn't look like my father.

There was a man leaving Paco's apartment when I got
there. An elegant older man who reeked of cologne and had
skin darker than mine. Paco didn't bother introducing us and
the man averted his face and left without saying goodbye. Paco
locked the door behind him. Then turned to me, all business.

Where's Louie? Isn't Louie with you?

No.

It's kind of late. What's your pleasure, Nick? Coke? Crack?

You seem pissed off.

I'm not.

I'll leave if you want.

You can stay or you can go. It's a free country, Nick.

Did I interrupt something? That guy—

What guy?

Who was just here.

Rodel? He's my lola's DI. You know what "DI" stands for
in this town? Dance instructor. That's code for gigolo, if you
haven't guessed.

Your lola sounds interesting.

Paco burst out laughing. Oh she is. Believe me, she is.

He lit a cigarette for me, then for himself. Then he sauntered
over to a cabinet and brought out a bottle of Patrón. He turned
off his cell phone and put on some painful, sexy song by Nina
Simone. We sat across from each other in the dimly lit mess of
a living room and smoked and drank, playing staring games and
prolonging the inevitable. Then Paco brought out the coke, cut-

ting fat lines on a mirror. I thought about saying no. Getting up and making my grand exit. I had to show up for work in a few hours. When I didn't move, Paco bent over the table and did a couple of lines. Then handed me the rolled-up thousand-peso bill and said, It's a free country, Nick.

THE DISAPPEARED

Ours was a dark, dirty, thrilling secret. Not even Louie knew. Though he wasn't a total fool and probably smelled that something was up. Now here's the thing: Paco didn't want to be seen with me in public; he'd made it perfectly clear. There was the issue of swanlike Gala, who he referred to—unironically—as "my fiancée." There was the issue of his snotty associates. And underneath it all, I knew, there was the issue of me being who I was. But what the fuck, I kept telling myself. The coke was free and the sex was good. Did I hate him? You bet. Did I love him? You bet.

Then one day Paco disappeared, just like that. He didn't call or text me back. Or Louie, or anyone else. I drove to his apartment in Malate one night after work. Sat outside like an idiot in my sad-ass car for hours, hoping he'd show up. My cell was on vibrate. Louie texted, then Tita Moning. I ignored them. By the time I got back to my aunt's house, my father was dead.

CHISMIS

According to Louie, Paco owed some psycho Muslims in Caloocan and had to leave town. Or maybe it was some psycho cop in Precinct Five, or maybe some psycho military guy from Camp Aguinaldo. The gist of it was Paco had burned his suppliers and made them very angry. The chismis got wilder. His Range Rover had been found abandoned in Pagsanjan. A burned-out shell, picked clean by thieves. There were Paco sightings in Baguio, Palawan, Bangkok, Sydney, and Amsterdam. Gala's father, who was high up in government and therefore privy to really inside shit, told her that Paco's mutilated corpse had just been found floating in the Pasig. And that, furthermore, Paco's pretty green eyes had been scooped out with a spoon.

We were at the Starbucks in Rockwell, where Louie and Gala liked to hang out, order mocha Frappuccinos, and be *seen*. Gala seemed pretty spooked. She kept looking from me to Louie. *It can't be true, right? Just my father and his chismis. Paco's alive. Hiding out until it's safe to come back. Nothing will ever happen, no matter who's been double-crossed. Not with that family of his. They'll always protect him. Right?*

She was weeping softly now. People at the other tables were turning to gawk at us. I handed her a bunch of paper napkins. Louie looked uneasy and patted her hand. He asked if she wanted another Frappuccino. He sure did. And maybe a croissant. Then he turned to me. What about you, Nick? Another espresso? I shook my head. Gala stopped crying long enough to say she was badly in need of some coke. Did Louie have any? Louie shook his head. Gala didn't bother asking me. She depended on Paco, she said. For her coke, for her fun, for her *everything*. And who was she supposed to depend on now?

SUNDAY, SIX P.M.

It was raining and I almost didn't recognize him. He was huddled in the doorway of this skeevy noodle joint in Binondo, the kind of skeevy joint in a skeevy alley where you wouldn't expect to see a guy like Paco. Or maybe you would. I pulled up and he got in the Corolla. The air-con wasn't working, but I had made sure to clean the car before picking him up.

We're going to my house in Forbes Park. McKinley Road, right by the Polo Club. You know how to get there, or shall I drive? His tone was curt. It reminded me of the way Louie talked to his driver.

Paco's hair was cut short and dyed black. His clothes smelled funky, like he'd been living in them a long time.

I miss you, I said, which was a big mistake.

He kept jiggling his right knee and staring straight ahead.

I'm glad you're not dead, I said. Another big mistake.

Just get me to Forbes Park in one piece, Nick. That's all I ask.

Traffic was insane. Everybody either coming from or going to church, or heading out to have some big Sunday-night family dinner.

Coño, Paco kept muttering. *Coño, coño, coño.*

We were stalled at the world's longest light. A ghostly beggarwoman and her baby appeared at my window. The woman's face dripping with rain. She held an open tube of Rugby up to her baby's nose. The baby wrapped in rags and not moving. It was either a doll or it was dead.

How much should I give her? I asked Paco, suddenly panicky.

Ignore her, Paco said.

I can't.

Try, Paco said. He kept checking his phone.

The light finally changed. The woman snarled at me and ran back to the median. I stepped on the gas.

Legacy

Funny, how Forbes Park is a gated community except for McKinley Road. Funny, considering who lives there. Paco's grandmother, for one thing. And other old-money families, richer and even more venerable than his. Dynastic fortunes made from shipping, from sugar, abaca, timber, copra, steel. And owning vast tracts of land, soaked in bloody history.

The house was hidden from the road by a high fence topped by barbed wire and jagged pieces of glass. There used to be a guard at the gate named Dionisio, Paco said. But he got busted trying to sell my lola's missing diamond necklace. Turned out he and one of the maids were robbing her blind.

He got out of the car and slipped his small hand—one of his least attractive traits—between the wrought-iron bars of the front gate and slid open the latch. I parked the car under an enormous acacia tree. The rain had stopped and the ground was muddy. We walked up to the entrance of the dark, sprawling house. I was nervous and starting to regret that I had come. Paco pressed the buzzer.

Back in the good old days, he said, you'd hear the intercom crackle before Miss Aguilar's voice piped up: *May I help you?*

Miss Aguilar was Lola Conching's secretary, and English was the language meant to put you in your place. It didn't matter if you were a fucking *taho* vendor or a fucking congressman, or some high-society matron who played mah-jongg with my lola on Saturday afternoons. You had to announce yourself to Miss Aguilar and get ready to wait.

And so we waited.

Don't you have a key? I asked him.

My lola had the locks changed when she kicked me out, Paco said. He pressed the buzzer again. When there was still no answer, he banged on the carved molave door with his fist. I thought I heard the faraway sound of a lost dog barking in a dream. My own fist throbbed with pain as I watched Paco bang on the heavy door.

It finally opened a crack. A man's gravelly voice said in disgust, Oh, it's *you.*

Paco pushed the door open and headed for the stairs, me attempting to follow. The man blocked our path.

You're not supposed to be here, he said.

I recognized Rodel, the man I'd run into leaving Paco's apartment. He and Paco were staring at each other with hatred. Rodel wore a robe over his fancy pajamas and looked very much at home.

Get out of my way, Paco said, trying to get past him. This is my house.

You mean your lola's, Rodel shot back. He grabbed Paco by the arm to stop him from going any farther. You can't go up there. She's had enough of you.

And you? Paco asked, leaning in and never taking his eyes off Rodel's face. Their lips close enough for a kiss. Have you had enough of me?

Your lola's not well, Rodel said in a quiet voice. You and your friend should leave, before you get us all killed.

Paco wrenched his arm free. Then pulled a knife and stabbed Rodel in the neck.

I didn't see where the knife came from, didn't see Paco whip it out of his jean jacket, his boot, wherever he was hiding it. Blood was spurting out of Rodel and I remember screaming like a girl. He died without making a sound. Paco ran up the stairs and didn't bother to look back at what he had done. I scrambled after him, not wanting to be left behind with Rodel's corpse. Statues of angels and saints leered down at us from their recessed shrines along the stairway.

Lola Conching, an ancient crocodile of a woman, was propped up in her massive bed watching television. One bejeweled hand clutching the remote, the other a flute of chilled vodka. She didn't seem surprised to see us. The air-con was humming, the lamps were lit, the news was on. More beheadings in Basilan by the Abu Sayyaf. Paco flopped down next to her and rested his head on her shoulder. I noticed the blood on Paco's shirt and wondered if she did too.

You need a bath, hijo, Lola Conching said. Then she said: What happened to your hair?

You shouldn't watch this depressing shit, Lola. You'll have nightmares, Paco said.

The old woman sipped her vodka. You know I like to keep informed. Would you rather I watch a Koreanovela?

I miss you, Lola. I miss you so much, Paco said.

Lola Conching stroked his head. This went on for some time. Then she said: You need money? You're always in trouble and you always need money. She took note of me standing there with a stunned expression. What's wrong with your friend?

He needs a drink, Paco said. And so do I.

You know where everything is. Help yourselves. I've fired all the maids. Or maybe you boys haven't noticed?

The bottle of Absolut was in a minifridge next to her dressing table. We each took swigs.

Do you remember when your Lolo Ramon was kidnapped on his way home from the airport? Lola Conching asked Paco, muting the volume but keeping her eyes fixed on the screen. It was midnight when he landed on the last plane from Hong Kong. Remember? They were waiting for him on the highway. Shot Peping. You remember Peping? A nice bodyguard, very polite. Anyway, they shot Peping five or six times, then the driver. Then cut their throats. Overkill, *talaga*. It was all over the news. You must've been nine or ten—

Five, Paco said. I was five.

The gang held your lolo hostage for over two weeks, the old woman continued. Terrible times, so much drama. I was convinced that everyone was in cahoots, including the cops. A lot of people hated your grandfather. And do you know why?

Because he was a son of a bitch and not afraid of anyone, Paco answered. Like you.

I paid the ransom, the old woman said. Like I was supposed to. After the cops brought your lolo home—the same cops who probably kidnapped him—I said to your mother, *They'll kidnap you and your son next. Or me. Mark my words.*

Mom wasn't there, Paco said.

Lola Conching tore her eyes away from the television. What?

Dead from an overdose the year I turned two. Just like my father.

Is that so? The old woman didn't seem convinced.

Lolo bought you a gun, Paco said. I remember that.

That's right. A 9mm. Glock.

Why'd you move him in?

Who?

Rodel.

The old woman shrugged. You have to understand, *hijo*. When your grandfather died, a sort of madness set in. I had the security system deactivated and fired everyone—Miss Aguilar, the driver, the gardener, the cook, the *labandera*, the—

Then you went dancing, Paco said.

I felt liberated! Ballroom, cha-cha, tango—

Then you moved him in.

That's right. Rodel's good company. Makes me laugh. He cooks for me. Sings to me. Sometimes he even does my hair.

People are after me, Lola. I need your help.

The woman's gaze shifted from Paco to me. Where's Rodel?

People are after me, Paco repeated. I need money. My money. All of it.

What money? It's all been spent.

What do you mean, it's all been spent?

Squandered, the old woman said. By you and everyone else in this cursed house.

They're going to kill me, Paco said.

Me! Me! Me! You brought this upon yourself. Suffer the consequences.

I'm your grandson. Your only heir.

His grandmother was unmoved. Stop being so sentimental and self-pitying. It doesn't suit you. Everything that's wrong with this country is rooted in greed, cheap emotion, and the Catholic Church. It's destroying us. There is no money left. Where's Rodel? What have you done to him?

I grabbed Paco by the arm. Let's go, I said.

HAPPY ENDINGS

In the first version, a lightbulb goes off in the old woman's head. She grabs her gun from under a pillow and shoots Paco. Not once, but twice. He's thrown back against the wall and slides down into a sitting position. The walls and ceiling are splattered with blood and bits of him.

Do you believe in God? Lola Conching asks, after a few moments have passed.

I don't know, I say. Then I throw up.

Paco's green eyes are open and amazed. Lola Conching never leaves her bed. She turns up the volume and stares at the television. A movie comes on. Some comedy from the '70s, starring Dolphy.

When I'm done throwing up, Lola Conching says: Get out of here, young man. Save yourself.

In the second version, Granny pulls out her Glock but doesn't shoot him. I grab Paco's arm and we hurry down the stairs, slipping on the bloody floor, stumbling over Rodel's splayed corpse as we run out into the night. Paco won't get in the car.

This is my house! Paco howls, staggering around the garden of orchids, palmyra, and bamboo. My house! My money!

The dogs of Forbes Park howl back at him in response. It's almost funny. I glance back at the house before getting in my car. The lights go out in the old woman's bedroom. And I leave Paco behind, and drive as fast and as far as I can in a last-ditch attempt to save myself. It starts to rain.

DESIRE

BY MARIANNE VILLANUEVA

Ermita

Which parts of a bird are edible?

Epifanio did not know.

He would guess. Yes, he could do that: Not the internal organs. Not the beak. Not the feathers.

He wrote, laboriously: *eyes, tail, breast*.

Afterward, when they were all gathered in the small lobby, they were offered warm Coke in thick glasses, no ice.

Why would anyone ask them a question about birds? They were there to study to be seamen: most of them were from Negros, like Epifanio. The rest were from Marinduque, Zambales, Cagayan de Oro, Davao. After two years on one of the interisland ferries, and provided they received good evaluations, they might get the chance to work on one of the cruise ships that went to Hong Kong and Singapore. Epifanio clung to this hope.

He liked the young woman who had been waiting to greet them the day they arrived in Manila, but there was no sign of her the next day, or the next. By the third day, he began to notice a fat man who sat in a little room on the first floor. The room had desks and filing cabinets, like a regular office. Epifanio learned later that the man's name was Leandro.

Epifanio pretended that the young woman had lent him some toothpaste and he wanted to repay her. "Is she coming back?" he asked Leandro.

The man smirked. "She's sick. Morning sickness. What's

your name again?" Epifanio gave his name. The man gazed down at a sheet divided into two columns. "From Bacolod," he said, and smirked again.

"Silay," Epifanio said. *And,* he thought, but didn't say aloud, *I have been to college. I have had two years of San Agustin. And you—!* He lowered his gaze and shrugged and gave a self-deprecating smile.

When Epifanio later replayed the conversation in his head, he hated the way Leandro seemed to know instinctively what Epifanio was after. And Leandro's smirk would return again and again to his memory.

The rules of being a seaman: The shared toilets must be cleaned and ready for inspection at five a.m. When a passenger requests assistance, the seaman must smile and show his willingness to be of service. Even the most unreasonable guest will appreciate a smile.

Manila, this teeming city, pressed on him: dense, impenetrable. The sounds were many and various and ill-tempered. They abated only a little, toward dawn. His eyes were heavy from his dreams. *Sheryn, I love you,* he would dream himself saying aloud. In the dream she always laughed, as if she could hear him speaking, even across so many islands. *I love you, I love you, I love you,* he would say, his fists clutching the thin mattress.

On the sixth day, there was no one in the little office. Papers were scattered on the floor. The filing cabinet drawers hung open. The desk had been overturned. A policeman stood by a window, speaking into a cell phone.

Epifanio stared. He thought he heard the policeman say, "*Ngunit*"—But—and then, "*mga estudyante.*" Epifanio did not want to listen anymore and turned away.

He found a few of the men gathered by the front door,

whispering urgently to one another. Epifanio forced himself to approach.

As he took a step forward, and then another, he felt a slickness on his shoes. He looked down, and dully noted that something dark seemed to have smeared the soles of the sneakers that were practically brand new, bought from Gaisano Mall the day before he left Bacolod. He didn't understand. His thoughts were slow. Perhaps that was Sheryn's laugh he had heard, ringing in his head when he reached the urgently whispering men.

"Epifanio!" said Benedicto, the big man from Murcia. "Did anyone tell you what happened?"

Sheryn's laugh was almost ear-splitting. The day was just beginning, but already he detested and feared it.

"Gonzago here thinks he heard something," said another man, the one Epifanio knew only as Baby. Epifanio had overheard some of the men gossiping about Baby. It was strange: he had angered his in-laws by slapping his wife, and they had made it impossible for him to remain in his own home, constantly abusing Baby in front of his own children.

Gonzago was old, almost forty. Everyone knew he roamed the halls in his sleep.

"If I did hear something," Gonzago said, "it wouldn't have helped. I might have heard the man's soul leaving his body, yes. It sounded like water slipping down a riverbank." Gonzago gestured, his right arm driving cleanly through the air.

Only then did Epifanio realize that the floor of the lobby was covered with the same dark substance that stained the soles of his sneakers. It was everywhere. There was even some of it smeared across one of the lobby's light blue walls. He saw what might have been a handprint.

Spit was collecting at the back of Epifanio's mouth. He swallowed, then managed to ask, "Who found him?"

* * *

Sheryn said, "I'm in love with Julio. He will make a better father to my child." Epifanio closed his eyes. When he opened them again, everyone but Gonzago had left. Gonzago was chuckling to himself. "Eh? The police ask so many questions. But all the wrong ones."

Epifanio turned from him and walked out the door.

"Eh?" Gonzago called after him. "No one is supposed to leave. The police are still taking statements."

Epifanio kept going. The street began less than a yard away. Here were spit stains on the buckling asphalt, and horrendous smells. There was almost no sidewalk to speak of. Banana peels, empty soda bottles, scraps of paper all formed a clotted mess in the gutters.

God is love, God is love, God is love. Epifanio trembled: Sheryn's pet mynah bird knew only this one sentence. Every time Epifanio called on her, the bird would direct a baleful glance at him and begin its monotonous chant.

There was a small orchard of cherisa trees behind Sheryn's house. He remembered going there with her, the taste of the small, tart fruit in her mouth, and then his.

Epifanio was not physically strong. He was a rather small man, with a slim waist. His forearms were corded from years of having worked as a welder at the sugar plant in Victorias. Six months earlier, he had been let go. The foreman refused to give him a reason.

To dream! Ah yes, he had dared to dream. The news spread quickly in the town. He slunk along the seafront, drinking bottle after bottle of San Miguel. When he next saw Sheryn, it was on the arm of another man. There was only the smallest hint of a bulge, beneath her waist. Only someone looking for it would have noticed.

Julio was tall and fair-skinned. He spoke good English. He worked in the business office of L'Fisher Hotel, one of the best hotels in Bacolod.

Epifanio's eyes reddened. *My child!* he thought. *Mine! Mine! Mine!*

Was Epifanio sorry about the fate of the smirking man? Naturally, yes. But he was also a little tense. Epifanio had disliked the man; it was this that made the guilt grow. Could his thoughts have somehow assumed a walking shape and descended from his room to the first floor, where the smirking man sat nodding off behind the desk in the small office?

Was Epifanio interested in the young woman because she reminded him a little of Sheryn? They had the same kind of hair: long and shiny, a treasure of fragrance. Sheryn was a little shorter. She also had a more winning manner, a more inviting smile.

But the young woman had not exactly been a closed door. This, at least, was the implication of the smirk that had accompanied the dead man's comment about "morning sickness."

But—was he really dead? What if he had merely been wounded, and the ambulance had rescued him in time? What if, even now, he was lying in some hospital, with a drip affixed to one arm?

Was *he* the father of the young woman's baby? Epifanio was surprised at the despair that accompanied this thought.

To hold a woman, any woman—to know the warmth of a woman's embrace.

Epifanio's parents had loved each other with a purity and single-mindedness that he had tried to emulate. But the ferocity of Sheryn's desire had unmanned him. They had been classmates in high school but Epifanio never dreamed of courting her. Then, one day in October, right in the middle of the Masskara Festival, she came up to him in the plaza. "*Gusto mo ako?*" she asked. Her tone was teasing. "*O, tilawi!*" Just like that.

During their first time together, she had grabbed him by the root and drawn him close. She had called up his courage and he had done things to her that he had never thought himself capable of. She had pulled him further into her, spreading her thighs wide, luxuriating in his desire. Her lips, Epifanio noticed, swelled with her arousal; her breasts too. He liked to hold one in each hand. They were not large, but they were all he needed.

When Epifanio and Sheryn encountered each other on the street, they feigned aloofness. Her family was not rich, but they were better off than Epifanio's; his father eked out a hard living as a fisherman. Epifanio had done many things: he had been a tricycle driver. Also, a waiter. Also, a traffic enforcer. Sheryn had graduated from college, whereas Epifanio had dropped out after two years. She worked as a teller in a bank, and wore nice clothes to work every day. Still, Sheryn wanted *him!* When they caught each other's eyes, they smiled surreptitiously, like conspirators.

Then, disaster: *I am carrying your child*, she whispered. The future shrank to the width of one hand. Her desire seemed to wither. There was a new kind of hard determination in her face. He talked of marriage; she said, *Wait*.

Sheryn's voice was strong near the bar. A sign said, *Deep and Deeper*. Epifanio had passed it before, had noticed the women going in and out, he knew what for. The women wore tight clothes that emphasized every curve. They walked languorously, aware that men were watching.

Epifanio lurked about, throwing quick glances at the door. A tall man with a smooth-shaven head and tattoos running down both forearms stood just inside, where he might easily have been mistaken for a shadow. He uttered a warning to Epifanio, and made a derisive gesture with his hand. Epifanio walked quickly away, his thin shoulders hunched up and his hands jammed into the pockets of his jeans.

Epifanio easily found the bar again two nights later. There was some kind of program going on: he listened to the voice of a man reciting lewd jokes into a microphone. The bar seemed full: the laughs were raucous. A young woman kept going in, out, in, out. She was not pretty. She wore a silvery blouse that hugged her breasts and Epifanio appreciated the slimness of her waist. Only after she had gone back and forth several times did it dawn on Epifanio that she was aware of him, that she was perhaps interested in him. She stood on the sidewalk, peering down the street as if looking for someone. He watched her turn, this way and that. She wore gold sandals; her toenails were painted bright red. Because she was taking her time about going back inside, Epifanio had ample opportunity to devour her with his eyes, to imagine himself doing certain things with her. Now he was sure: she wanted him! But he could do nothing, only stand and stare.

She came out a third time and stood on the sidewalk. Her lips seemed brighter. No one else was on the street, or in the world: there was only the girl, and Epifanio, and his aching need. She turned in a slow semicircle. He knew she was urging him on, trying to arouse him to some form of action. His eyes took what they could.

When she had exhausted every possible movement, she turned and walked slowly back to the bar. Her head was held high, but Epifanio could sense her disappointment. He had saved her, or himself, he didn't know which.

It was his first time in Manila, but the city had always existed in his head. It was his last remaining opportunity, the one he would run to when everything else had failed, his last card. He didn't want to be playing that card so soon, but he found the situation with Sheryn unbearable. So, like a gambler, he had played it.

Epifanio went to see Sheryn one last time before leaving. His eyes were puffy and red. She looked at him and grazed his left cheek with the tips of her fingers. "Silly," she said softly. "Nothing to cry about. Silly, silly." Epifanio's gaze traveled to her stomach, the roundness there. That was when she pulled away, both hands over her belly as if protecting it. "You'd better leave." When he didn't move, she said, sharply, "Go!"

He rose, stiffly.

The men's breakfast was provided by the boardinghouse. For lunch and dinner, however, they had to spend their own meager funds. Someone told them that the food stalls near the bus terminals had the cheapest food. These usually served pork barbecue—ten pesos a stick—or "Adidas," chicken feet. The color of the meat made Epifanio want to retch.

For the past week, he had forced himself to last as long as possible on the breakfast: two small sausages, one egg, and a small pyramid of rice. By noon, he was faint. By dinnertime, he was angry. But he found a way to endure the hunger.

There had been no breakfast served that morning, because of the tragedy. The manager of the boardinghouse had paced the lobby, throwing curses right and left. His wife, who was in charge of the kitchen, moaned, *Dios mío, Dios mío*. One couldn't have asked about breakfast at such a time. Epifanio wandered the streets, willing himself into exhaustion.

Eventually, he found himself on the street with the bar. He waited. He felt like sinking down on the pavement, but looked in disgust at the gobs of spit that formed a dense pattern by the gutters. When the woman finally came out, she seemed to look for him. Her eyes found him, and he sensed the invitation and longing. He came forward.

"What's your name?" he asked. He spoke very softly, hoarse with fear and desire.

"Honey," she said, smiling. "What's yours?"

He shook his head and paused. Then he decided that she deserved to know at least this about him: "Epifanio," he said.

She kept smiling. She leaned against him. He could feel her small breasts, pressed against his chest. He raised his right arm to circle her waist.

"You like me?" she whispered.

He nodded. From his pocket, he pulled out all the money he had. She grabbed the bills eagerly and started to count. Then she said, "You rich? Did you really mean to offer this much?"

He didn't even know how much he had in his pocket. When did he get the money? This morning? He saw the eyes of the dead man. He stanched the memory.

"Yes, I meant to offer that much," he asserted. He felt manly now. Strong.

Honey laughed. "You can have me the whole night for this," she said.

Epifanio nodded. She drew him inside.

DARLING, YOU CAN COUNT ON ME

BY ERIC GAMALINDA

Santa Cruz

1. FROM THE MANILA TIMES

PAIR OF GIRL'S LEGS FOUND IN TRASH PILE

May 30, 1967. A garbage collector found a pair of legs, severed neatly into four parts at the knees and hip joints and wrapped in old newspapers, in a trash pile on Avenida Rizal, Santa Cruz, at 11:25 last night. Last week, a badly decomposed human hand was found in front of a barbershop on Recto Avenue. Is anybody missing a sister, daughter, or niece—about 18 or 20?

GIRL'S HEADLESS BODY IDENTIFIED

May 31, 1967. Police investigators last night established the identity of the woman whose headless body was found in a vacant lot on Epifanio de los Santos Avenue yesterday afternoon. The dead woman's fingerprints matched police files of Lucila Lalu, 29. Detectives said a pair of legs found yesterday in a trash can on Avenida Rizal also belonged to Miss Lalu, owner of the Pagoda Cocktail Lounge and Lucy's House of Beauty in Santa Cruz. A coroner said the woman had just given birth.

LUCILA LALU SLAY SUSPECT HELD

June 1, 1967. Police last night detained the alleged paramour of Lucila Lalu, whose headless body was found Tuesday evening. However, Florante Relos, 19, who admitted being the lover of Miss Lalu, was released after he gave what police thought was an "airtight" alibi—on the night of the murder, he had been drinking with three friends, who corroborated his story. Relos said that Miss Lalu had wanted to break up with him and that he had stopped seeing her two weeks ago.

COPS TAG LUCILA KILLER!

June 6, 1967. Manila police have tagged Patrolman Aniano de Vera as a principal suspect in the murder of Lucila Lalu. Police believe Officer de Vera, Miss Lalu's husband of seven years, had "the strongest motive"—jealousy. De Vera recently discovered that Miss Lalu had been having an affair with Florante Relos, a waiter at her cocktail lounge.

LUCILA KILLER CONFESSES!

June 15, 1967. Unburdening himself of the weight of his guilt, Jose Luis Santiano, married and father of five, submitted a handwritten confession to police authorities. Santiano, a boarder on the mezzanine above Lucila Lalu's beauty parlor in Santa Cruz, said Miss Lalu tried to seduce him in his bedroom at around 11:30 p.m. last May 28, and that he strangled Miss Lalu during a "mental blackout."

"I DID NOT KILL HER!"

June 18, 1967. Jose Luis Santiano last night retracted his previous confession that he killed Lucila Lalu and claimed, instead, that he was an unwilling witness to the murder by three men. These men allegedly instructed him to admit to the murder and claim Miss Lalu tried to seduce him. They also warned him not to tell anybody about the murder. Mean-

while, investigators say the latest piece of evidence against Santiano is a ball-peen hammer found on a ledge of his mezzanine apartment. Is Santiano lying? Was he paid to confess? Did he participate in the crime?

2. FLORANTE'S VERSION

First of all, she wouldn't change the lock on him. That is so beneath her. He tries his key again. It gets stuck in the lock, and he tries to wiggle it free. No use. Aniano must have done it. The man is a pig and a snake. *Baboy na, ahas pa.* No wonder she hasn't fucked him in years. The very idea makes him want to puke.

He looks up. The sky is a churning mass of gray. *Bruise-colored* is the way she likes to describe it, just before it rains. She said a poet taught her that. From the corner of his eye he can see flickering lights where the alley opens up to Avenida Rizal. The sun has just set. Its last faint light glimmers like tinsel peeling off the sides of jeepneys as they careen through the avenue. *Glimmers*: maybe if he started talking like a poet she would change her mind. *Like tinsel:* that must be a good sign. God has given him a sign. If God lets him get to her before she does it, if he can stop her somehow . . .

But she couldn't have changed the lock on him. He tiptoes to look in through the shop window, the bottom half of which is boarded up. He's not very tall. She once made a remark about that. He was hurt, and she never said it again. He can see part of the shop where he helped her install a red leatherette sofa just a month ago. It was going to be her new reception area, where the ladies of the Pagoda Cocktail Lounge could read the latest gossip magazines while they waited for their turn to get their hair teased or their nails done. Red for good luck, just like the Chinese *siopao* vendors along the avenue told her. *I believe in the signs,* he says to himself. *Give me a sign, and I will believe.*

He can see her lying on the sofa, her forearm resting over her eyes, her legs stretched across a pool of shiny red. He can see her so clearly: there's a run in her stocking, revealing a pale slice of skin. He taps on the window. She's barely breathing. He taps again, softly at first, then louder and more insistently. She must be fast asleep. Odd to do that at this hour, so early in the evening, when a stray hostess with an emergency—a broken nail, a wealthy date who wants her hair done a certain way—might just pop in, breathless and frantic and needing her help.

Maybe she already did it. But she wouldn't get rid of her baby just because she's seeing another boy. And she wouldn't desert him for another boy. *You are far too pure for that*, he finds himself whispering as he taps on the window again. The light of the lamppost across the street hisses, sputters, then goes out. The alley is totally dark now. He looks at his watch. He has spent an entire hour trying to get in. The sky looks like it's about to fall. It's too early for rain. Rain doesn't come till June. Not till next week.

He looks in again. She has put her arm down, but her eyes are still shut. He taps and taps but she does not move. And then, for some reason, something in him sinks. He feels the weight bearing down on him. He knows the sky is going to break and rain will fall, early and bizarre. Maybe she's already done it. This cannot be undone. God has given him a sign. God is telling him he has come too late. God wants to get drunk with him. God is saying that forgetting is as easy as a case of beer. *I'll drink a case with You, God, so I'll have the guts to tell You to go to hell.*

3. Aniano's Version

She lies down on the sofa and shuts her eyes. "Look what you've done," she says. "There's a run in my stocking."

"You can barely see it," he says.

"You hit me again, Aniano, I swear I'll walk out on you."

"I didn't hit you. I just pushed you a little."

"I can't go out now."

"Just take it off then," he says. "It's a birthday party. At a fucking Chinese restaurant. What do you need to wear stockings for?"

"Nobody goes anywhere without stockings."

"Sure, you want to look nice for the birthday boy."

"For heaven's sake, Aniano. The guy's a fag."

"Yeah? With a wife and five kids. Pretty macho for a fag, no? Is that his room up there? How much do you charge him? Or maybe he's getting free rent himself, like that teenage lover of yours. You like them young, no? Young and *promdi*. Just like you."

Her eyelids flutter for an instant, the way they always do when she doesn't know what to say. They remind him of butterflies. Black butterflies, which are bad luck.

"Stop staring at me," she says.

"Give me the key to the front door."

"Can't."

"Because you gave the copy to your teenage boyfriend?"

"Because I only have one key."

"All locks come with duplicate keys. Any idiot knows that."

"Fine. You be the brilliant detective. Go to that hardware store and ask Mr. Cheng why he gave me only one key. Maybe he's fucking me too, right?"

"Maybe."

"You're so sick, Aniano."

He keeps staring at her. She's wearing her favorite dress, a silk orange shift that sort of matches the streaks of color in her hair. She lifts her eyelids slightly, the black gash of mascara splitting open to reveal just the whites of her eyes.

"Oh, you're still here," she says wearily.

"Why is your hair turning that way?"

"What?"

"It's turning orange. Like rust."

"I like it this way."

"I like it too."

"Sure."

"Does he like it that way?"

"Oh, for heaven's sake, Aniano."

"Bet he loves to touch it."

"He loves to shampoo and blow-dry and tease it like I am fucking Audrey Hepburn. Satisfied?"

He comes closer, hovering over her. "Is the apartment nice?"

"What apartment?"

"The apartment you got for that teenage waiter of yours. I heard it was nice. In Cubao, even. Pretty fancy!"

"*Puta*, Aniano, I can't keep track of who you're being jealous of."

"You tell me. How many boys are you fucking anyway?"

"Three hundred and sixty-five, okay? One for each day of the year. Leap years I take a day off."

That gives him some pause, to her relief. "Your lipstick matches the color of the sofa," he says.

"Inborn talent."

"He picked that for you, that color lipstick? You never wore red lipstick before. You always wore pink. Red is for hookers."

"So now I'm a hooker."

"So, what about the apartment?"

"What about it?"

"Is he keeping the love nest?"

"He can keep it for as long as he can pay the rent."

"You mean *you*. For as long as *you* can pay the rent."

She bolts up. He steps back, taken by surprise, his hand instinctively gripping the revolver on his hip.

"*Puta*, Lucila, don't move like that. I could have shot you."

"Sure, just shoot me and get it over with. I told you it's all over. He's out of my life. What more do you want?"

"Yeah? He was here earlier, you know. Trying to pick the lock like a two-bit thief. Why didn't you let him in? No time for a little quickie tonight? Got other plans?"

"Oh God, shoot me now."

"I will too, you know."

She walks toward him. "Why don't you?" Her lips are close enough to brush against his. "Can you stand losing this?"

He looks straight in her eyes. Under the glare of the fluorescent light they seem darker than he's ever noticed before, a deep, *barako* black.

"Go ahead," she taunts him. "Can you stand never seeing these eyes again? Never touching me again?" She takes his hand and holds it over her breasts. "Can you stand never seeing these beauties again?" She leads his hand farther down. "Or this?"

"Goddamn you, Lucila," he says. "And your teenage boyfriend."

She throws her head back and laughs. "Go, run after him. He's probably still out there, that little dog. You boys just go and shoot each other up, like cowboys and injuns. There, can you see? He's out there trying to get in. Go get him, Aniano. Hop along, cowboy."

He opens the door and peers out. "Lamppost blew out again," he says. "Cheap bulbs from fucking Japan. Total losers, those *sakang*. What time are you coming home?"

"I'll come home when I come home. Business is business."

He can't get himself out the door. "I don't hate you, Lucila."

"*Basta*."

"I think you are a good woman, but you have been misled."

"What, you turning evangelical now?"

"You were so—*good*—when I first met you. So virginal."

"All things must pass."

"Fallen from grace. Led astray by those reckless boys. By this dump of a neighborhood. You should move out of Santa Cruz. Santa Cruz is for losers. All migrants and students and hookers and addicts."

"It gets the money in. Can't say the same for your job. Why don't you take a few more bribes, like everyone does? Maybe then I'll think of moving my shop. Makati, how does that sound? Tease the hair of all them rich *matronas*. Or what about Malacañang? Maybe do Imelda's hair. How about that?"

He can still hear her talking as he finally walks out. He turns toward Avenida Rizal and its vertiginous frenzy, jeepneys speeding past and barely missing the hawkers who have spread out their goods on the sidewalk, socks and underwear, flashlights and knives. He suddenly feels revolted by all the commotion. He enters an alley and continues walking until he is deep in the labyrinth of the neighborhood. In this warren of dimly lit alleys, open canals run along the length of the sidewalks, black soupy water gurgling through. He keeps walking until he realizes he has lost his way. Only a few of the wooden two-story houses are illuminated with bare incandescent bulbs, which he can see through wooden grills. *Dormitories*, he tells himself, *prison cells, what's the difference?* For some years now their owners have been partitioning these family homes into cheap rooms where students from the provinces board for years, hoping to get a better life in Manila. Now Santa Cruz is the dormitory capital of the Philippines—you got to be famous for something, right? Lucila used to live in one of those rooms until he took her away. *Morons, there's no better life here. Unless you have an ass like my wife, the joke's on you.* He can hear the words growling inside his head, so loud they seem to be coming from somewhere else. Then he finds himself on a dead-end street, and at the other end, backed against a cement wall, is a stray dog as large as a bull, frothing at the mouth, cornered and growling and ready to pounce on him.

"You'll be dinner for someone else," he says. "Not me. Not this time."

The dog lurches forward, barking.

"Fuck off," he says. He pulls out his revolver and fires a shot. The blast hurls the dog backward, leaving a spray of blood on the wall.

4. JOSE'S VERSION

He can hear them whispering in the parlor below.

He can hear him telling her how long he'd been waiting, and how he was afraid it would rain. She silences him with a kiss. He can hear their mouths coming together, the soft moan that escapes from his throat as she presses her lips against his.

He climbs out of bed and lies flat on the floor. He presses his ear against the wooden floorboards. The ceiling fan whirring right beneath his ear muffles the sound a little, but he can still hear everything clearly. It feels like he's right in the room with them.

She's saying, *No, not now, it still hurts.*

But you want it to hurt.

Not like this. How would you feel if you were the one getting hurt?

Long silence. There's the sound of a plastic bottle cap being opened, and something thick and liquid being squirted out. He can hear him moan again. He's saying, *Okay, show me.*

Does it hurt now?

Yes, he says.

Stop?

No. You use this a lot?

Only when I'm lonely.

He presses his ear flat against the floorboards. Now he can hear even the slightest whisper. *You want to know what it really feels like?* her voice taunting and tender at the same time. *I'll push it all the way in.*

He closes his eyes and presses his lips against the floor. He can taste dust and wax. They're silent again. Then he can hear someone in the shower, the water a slow and steady trickle. He slips his hand in his shorts. He comes almost instantly. He feels a deep and comforting solace, like the first few moments after a typhoon. He feels grateful for this stillness. He wants to disappear in it.

Suddenly the door bursts open.

"*Anak ng puta.*" Lucila is standing at the door. She's wearing lace panties and a matching bra. She walks straight in as he struggles to get up. "You're going to get this floor waxed from now on," she says. "I'm sick and tired of you messing on my floor."

"I must have fallen asleep," he says. "I must have fallen out of bed."

"The fuck you did." She sits down on the bed. "Who do you jack off to? I hope it's me."

"You know it's you."

"You don't do it when Florante fucks me. Or Aniano. Just him." She picks up the Marlboros on his desk and taps the bottom of the pack to push a stick out, which she removes with her lips. "Don't look so surprised, Joey. I can hear every move you make." Her lips are bloodred and there's a streak of lipstick across her left cheek. "You miss your wife?"

"Not anymore."

"You jack off to her too?"

"That's the way he does it," he snaps.

"What?"

"To get a smoke out of the pack. That's the way everyone in school does it." Then, after a few moments, "I've run out of matches."

She puts the cigarette down. "How much do you hear when you're lying down there?"

"Nothing."

"You got come trickling down your leg," she says. "That doesn't happen for no reason."

He reaches across her for a tissue and wipes himself dry.

"Another wasted moment," she sighs.

"I'm not going to do it again."

"Just clean up when you're done, okay? You can't help it. You're as horny as your friend. Birds of a feather."

"He's not my friend. We just met in school."

"Funny. Talks about you all the time."

"What does he say?"

"I think he's in love with you."

"He's in love with *you*. I'm not a homo."

"Never said you were." She's struggling to keep a strap from falling off her shoulder. "How was the party?"

"There was no party."

"You were here all night?"

"Correct."

"Because you knew he'd be here."

"I haven't been feeling well—"

"How come he only sees me at night, that friend of yours? He a vampire?"

"No."

"You a vampire?"

"No."

"You want to suck my blood?"

"No, of course not."

"Then what is it?"

"I think he's afraid he'll fall in love. If he sees you too often."

She laughs. "Too late for that. He's in love as a dog. *Darling, you can count on me.* He sings that to me when we fuck, you believe that? *Till the sun dries up the sea.*"

"He *sings?*"

"In my ear. Who says romance is dead? You know Don's going to be a father soon, right?"

"His name isn't Don."

"Whatever. That's what I like to call him. Don Everly. That's the cute one, no? I can never tell one from the other. Maybe you can teach him a few lessons. How to be a nice daddy. Just like you. You a nice daddy?"

"He's too young. Are you sure?"

"A woman knows, for heaven's sake."

"It could be someone else's."

"It's certainly not yours." Her bra finally unsnaps. Her left breast spills out. He can see a few cuts on it. "*Puta,*" she says. "Your friend bites too much. Look what he's done."

"I have a Band-Aid."

"Always the perfect accessory."

He rummages through a shelf above the sink. There's a Nescafé glass and cutlery and a kitchen knife. "I can't find it." He looks back and sees her massaging her breast.

"You like it?"

"Lucila, don't."

"Because you're *bakla.*"

"No."

She hooks the strap back on her shoulder. "Don't worry," she says. "I got rid of it."

"Of what?"

"Your friend's baby. Washed it down the drain. You know what it looks like when it's this early? Like you got a big-ass menstruation. Just a big dark blob of blood . . . Come here, Joey. I'm not going to steal your friend from you."

"I can't, Lucila."

"Give me one good reason."

"My friend's still downstairs."

"A threesome then. This is your lucky day."

"What did you do with him?"

"What?"

"You were doing something—*funny*. What did you do?"

"I share my toys with everyone, Joey. I'm a nice girl." And then she pauses, and it seems as if there's a light twinkling in her eyes. "Oh my God," she says. "You really are—he really is—oh, I get it now."

He walks to her and realizes he's still holding the knife in his hand and his hand is trembling and something warm is once again trickling down his leg. She notices it and sees the knife gleam and for some reason she finds it ridiculous and laughs that funny laugh again, throwing her head back. Her neck is long and white, and her laughter gurgles out warm and rippling like water, like she's choking on her own laughter. He drops the knife. He inches closer to her, closer to the source of that mysterious sound. He reaches out for her breasts, barely brushing his fingers against them, then suddenly clenches her throat, firmly squeezing it as he blacks out.

5. LUCILA'S VERSION

She's been having the weirdest dreams.

She's flying over the alleys of Santa Cruz, her arms spread out. It's not an astral experience. It's not her soul that's flying. The wind just picks her up, like debris, and there she is, skimming over the ramshackle dormitories, wobbly antennas spiked all over the tin roofs.

There's Florante on a street corner drinking with his buddies. She zooms in and sees his lips up close, the lips she liked to bite in the heat of the moment, savoring the taste of iron and salt. He's bawling his eyes out and cursing. He looks up and shakes his fist at her, at the sky, at the empty hole where God had been. *Drink up, You God, and go to hell.*

Now she can see Aniano lost in the warren of alleys and suddenly he's at Shoe World in Carriedo, watching as she tries on a pair of wet-look pumps. It's yesterday or the day before yesterday. When the saleslady brings the box over she clings to his arm and reminds him that there's a run in the toe of her left stocking, because he had pushed her and now he's sorry and he's buying her a new pair of shoes to make up. He slips her shoe off and takes her foot in his hand, the way the prince did with Cinderella. He tells her it feels like he's taking a rose, small and delicate, in his hand, and if he catches her with another boy again he's going to snap that foot off, like a flower.

Now she's with Joey in his room, and she's standing by the window, looking out at the churning sky. Rain tonight, early rain. He creeps behind her and wraps an arm around her belly and presses hard against her. With his other hand he jabs a knife into her heart. The pressure makes her gasp for air. An odor of iron permeates the room.

And now she's inside a flashback, just like those dreamy dissolves in the last feature show she watched at the Lyric on Avenida Rizal with Don, late at night in the back row of the balcony, when the ushers are too tired to stop them from petting. It's the first time she's met him, and Don is telling her something you wouldn't believe happened when Joey introduced them earlier that evening, something wide-screen and cinematic.

"That's what they all say, Don." The sound of her own voice surprises her. She can hear the words loud and clear, like they're resonating from her entire body.

"I knew I wanted you entirely," he says. "The way the devil wants our souls."

She laughs.

"Okay, you've heard it all before, but that's the way it is."

"Tell me one thing about me you'd kill for."

"The color of your hair."

"What?"

"I like looking at your hair when you suck my dick. It's like getting a blow job from Marilyn Monroe."

"The bitches at the Pagoda say it looks like cotton candy."

"It's the color of mandarin oranges."

"Mandarin oranges, *walanjo!* Nobody in that dive can tell a mandarin from a chink. Fill my head with words, you son of a bitch."

"I'll smooth-talk you and pillow-talk you. Be your own private José Corazón de Jesus, your own heart of Jesus."

"You scare me."

"Why?"

"You'll wind up like everybody else. That's how it all ends."

"Not me."

"Every man I've ever met reminds me of Manila's traffic."

"Explain."

"I never know which way to turn. There are no street signs, and everyone ignores the few that say *Stop* or *Yield*."

She closes her eyes and imagines it. Through this maze of dilapidated alleys and dead ends, there's nothing but long stretches of desolate highways, cities teeming with anonymous faces, restrooms that stink like a sewer, motels full of bugs where the walls still throb with love's sticky whispers, and always a lot of stations where people come and go. She wonders if he can see it too. Of course he can. Everything is transparent in a dream.

"Nobody ever gave you what you're looking for," he says.

"Bingo."

"Not me. With me, you know exactly where you're headed. You can see the end of the road. You always wanted it, the final fade-out. I'm going to take you there. I never break a promise."

It's the morning after, and she's brought him to her favorite fortune-teller, a creepy old widow in a shabby room above the Pagoda. The woman is telling them they're for keeps. Her voice is raspy, quivering. "What a wonderful message the cards have for you today, Lucila. There will be no other man in your life after him." He is her ace of wands, her flowering phallus, her other side of no tomorrow.

"Bullshit," she says. "But better than nothing."

Because that is what love is. Any fool can tell you this. It obliterates you completely, until there's only room for the beloved. Everything fades to black. It's like that wicked card the woman showed her, right after she first got off the bus in Manila, the armor-clad skeleton on horseback, the card of dying and rebirth. The woman kissed her palm: she had never seen a mound of Venus so clearly defined, had never met anyone whom the goddess of desire looked upon so enviously. *Lucila, you will be astonishing, novel, and meteoric.* A girl couldn't ask for more.

6. DON'S VERSION

Don steps out of the shower, a towel wrapped around his waist. She's nowhere to be found. He calls her name. No answer. He grabs his clothes and bolts up the stairs to Joey's room.

She's lying on the bed, Joey sitting next to her.

"Is she asleep?"

Joey shakes his head.

"*Coño*, Joey, you couldn't wait to do it downstairs?"

"She was going to tell everyone about me."

"*Putragis*, she ripped my T-shirt."

"Fucking blackmail."

"It's real Ban-Lon, *puñeta.*"

"What do we do now?"

"Made in fucking Hong Kong. You know how much this cost?"

"We'll get you another one, okay? You said you knew what to do."

"Let me think."

"Did you get the money?"

"*Nada.*"

"I told you to look in the cash box. She keeps everything in the cash box."

"I looked. There was nothing."

"It's not a robbery if nothing's stolen."

"Obviously."

"Well, this is really fucked."

"It *is* fucked, *puta.* You're so fucked."

"Maybe she's not really dead."

"She's dead, *bobo.* She's already starting to stink."

Suddenly Joey's bawling like a baby.

"*Leche*, Joey, not now."

"I wanted to do the right thing. I thought I was doing the right thing. Wasn't I doing the right thing?"

He puts his arm around Joey. "We'll think of something."

"I wanted to protect you."

"Not good, Joey. I can't be your alibi."

"Did you like her?"

"She liked me."

"She wanted to do it to me too."

"No kidding."

"That's why I did what I did."

"Son of a bitch. Two-timing slut. I should have known."

"I didn't lead her on or anything. I would never do that to you."

"I just turn around and she's already fucking my best friend."

"She was no good for you."

"Nor for you."

"I'm glad she's dead." Joey picks up the knife and holds it against her groin. "Don't look." He slides the knife quickly. A lip of muscle opens. A thick tongue of blood oozes out.

Don staggers. He leans against the wall.

Joey runs to him and holds him in his arms. "Go away. I'll take care of it."

"Do something about her eyes. Her eyes are open."

"No they're not."

"They're still kind of open, for heaven's sake."

"Okay. Am I really your best friend?"

"What?"

"You said I was your best friend."

"Yes, you are."

"Hey, you know something?"

"What?"

"It's my birthday."

"No kidding? Wow, *pare*. Happy birthday." He gives Joey a hug. "Do something."

As soon as he's gone, Joey notices that he's left drops of shower water on the floor, like little beads of glass. He stares at them for a while, wondering if he could pick them up. Maybe, if he was careful enough, he could even hold them up to the light.

7. Fade to Black

Don sleeps all the next day. He takes a shower, puts clean clothes on, and walks out. It must have rained nonstop. He has to inch his way along the sidewalk as passing jeepneys swell the flood-water and stir up muddy waves. Vendors along the sidewalk are pulling down plastic tarps, drenching passersby with torrents of water.

He's in a bar down the block from his apartment. It's happy hour. He's sitting by the window, looking out. The place is packed and noisy, full of people who have walked in to find a dry spot.

A man sitting at another table has been staring at him, his porcine face glowing with sweat, his coffee untouched and cold. Don stares back. The man doesn't blink, and finally speaks up.

"Hands and legs."

"Beg pardon?"

"They found a woman's hands and legs." He passes Don his copy of the *Manila Times*.

"It's the projects," Don tells him. "Folks there get butchered all the time."

"*Hindot!* Good thing we live in Santa Cruz."

"It could be anyone."

"Some people are real sloppy, *puta*." The man sucks on a cigarette and blows the smoke out, exhaling loudly, with exas-peration. "You really fucked up. I told you to make sure that sissy Florante would go back."

"He was too drunk to go back."

"You and your friend better think of a story fast." He gets up to leave.

"Aniano," Don says, "I'm getting out of here. I've had enough."

"Not till you finish the job."

"Joey will take care of it."

"Joey's going to crack the minute you leave." Aniano stubs the cigarette out on the table with a slight hiss. "If he does, you know what to do."

"He won't say a thing."

"How do you know?" He leaves.

Don waits a few minutes, then goes to the cashier to ask if he can use the phone. He calls a number. He doesn't have much to say. "Meet me at the bar. Right now."

He hangs up, pays the cashier ten centavos, and walks out. He stretches his arms. The sky is still overcast. He should have brought a jacket. He walks a few blocks toward Avenida Rizal, stops to purchase a ball-peen hammer from a sidewalk vendor, who wraps it in a thick roll of newspaper. Don continues walking down the avenue, then makes a sharp turn into an alley, pulls a key out of his pocket, and lets himself inside a building through the back door.

He's inside Lucila's House of Beauty. He bolts up the stairs to Joey's room. There's no one there either. He looks out the window into the street below. A vendor is passing by, balancing a bamboo pole with two baskets of duck eggs steaming on each end. As soon as the vendor is out of sight, Don drops the hammer onto the ledge. Then he walks out, heading back in the direction of the bar.

A block away he can already see Joey under the lamppost outside the bar. Joey's face is crunched, his hands shoved in his pocket. He looks like he's in tears. But when he sees Don his eyes suddenly beam. Maybe it's the light from the lamppost, a cataract of amber streaming down his face.

NORMA FROM NORMAN

BY JONAS VITMAN

Chinatown

She doesn't have to travel very far to see her fortune-teller. This is the chief advantage of living in the Chinese section of Manila known as Binondo. From her apartment on Espeleta, it's three quick blocks then up two flights of creaky wood stairs. On the third-floor landing, to announce her presence, she will call up to the woman who could be anywhere from forty to eighty and who, using the Fukienese word for grandmother, goes by the name Ah-ma.

Ah-ma is the trade secret of the girls in Charmaine's group.

Charmaine doesn't know why the Chinese make the best fortune-tellers. She has tried everyone else. There are the Catholic matrons, who are of two types: well-preserved socialites fallen on hard times; and the provincial transplants with their reedy bodies and brown-brown faces who consult in the front rooms of the overpopulated shacks they call home. A deck of playing cards is common to this type. There are also the *baklas* or homos she meets at the clubs—dabblers in trades from cosmetology to cosmology, whose instrument is the tarot. There are of course palm readers, tea readers, face readers, witch doctors who specialize in potions, spells, and counterspells, and two Americans who do extensive readings based on your horoscope—though Charmaine had inevitably run into the dilemma of not having the exact time of her birth, a very important detail to these specialists.

Ah-ma is the only Chinese fortune-teller Charmaine has

ever been to, but according to the girls in Charmaine's group, she is typical of the Chinese fortune-tellers in Manila, and by typical, it is understood that she is superior to all other non-Chinese practitioners.

Of course, these Chinese fortune-tellers are Buddhists and they conduct sessions in the halls and storefronts of their faith, places accoutred with wood and ceramic statues, depicting a celestial range from martial saints of protection with their slightly demonic faces and clutched weaponry to the hermaphroditic and peaceful face of Kwan Yin, the Buddhist goddess of mercy. Ah-ma's place of business, which is a floor below where she lives with her only remaining relative, a grandson of eight, has plenty of these statues, and needless to say, Charmaine's favorites are the various Kwan Yins, resting on the floor, by a couple of windowsills, and among the pantheon arrayed in a tiered central altar that also includes the commemorative black-and-whites in gold frames of the deceased relations of Ah-ma's various disciples and clients—a funerary memorial.

Charmaine also loves the smell of incense perpetually suffusing the air in Ah-ma's establishment. There is no Catholic equivalent in the churches she used to attend as a young believer—the burning candles had no fragrance to speak of, the incense was acrid like metal smoke, and the holy water no more than regular water that the priest was supposed to have transformed by passing his hand over it.

On the ground floor of Ah-ma's building is a hardware store called Happy Fortune Supply, and this too has convinced Charmaine of Ah-ma's superiority to all other seers, to Ah-ma's aptness in Charmaine's life.

The tubby eight-year-old grandson runs around the large altar as Charmaine and Ah-ma are consulting. He is like a miniature

Buddha. Fatness must run in the family: his grandmother is also a large person, and among the reasons Charmaine has difficulty discerning the woman's age is because the fat around her neck and on her face has stretched smooth any wrinkles, and because, encased in loose clothes, her body is voluminously formless.

Ah-ma goes into a trance, her eyes rolling back until they are merely whitish, quivering splotches on her face. This has always creeped Charmaine out, so she looks at the ground or at her own hands or at the table that sits between the two of them. Also, there is a low hum, a ululation that signals Ah-ma's possession by a spirit or spirits. For now, the grandson is a suitable alternative to Ah-ma's altered visage. He is playing peek-a-boo with Charmaine. She smiles at him. She wonders if he can tell what she is. She wonders, too, but less so, about Ah-ma; again, the fat peacefulness of that face makes any kind of emotion or judgment impossible to read.

Ah-ma makes a subtle transition back to her old self. She opens her eyes and smiles at Charmaine. Because her Tagalog is broken, Charmaine has to sometimes ask the woman to repeat what she's just said.

Before Ah-ma invoked the Buddhist spirit or spirits, she'd asked Charmaine to come up with a question. This is the question for which Ah-ma intercedes on Charmaine's behalf, conversing with the other world: *Will everything go all right over the next week?*

And the other world, through Ah-ma, has answered in the affirmative.

Charmaine hands over a one-hundred-peso bill. This is not payment. That's what Ah-ma says to all who come to her. By giving money, they are merely helping keep Ah-ma's temple clean, making sure there is always incense for the funerary pictures and gods of the altar, as well as offerings of siopao buns and hopia cakes, since hunger is the most marked characteristic of the dead and of the immortal.

Where is the grandson? Peek-a-boo! Out he comes from behind the skirt that wraps around the base of the altar, making the golden embroidered phoenixes and Chinese lettering on the cloth dance. Before Charmaine leaves, she fishes in her handbag for two sour ball candies. She hands them over to the fat grandson, the plastic wrappers making a noise.

Yes. Everything will go all right this week. But Charmaine, walking home, is not assured. Why should she disbelieve Ah-ma now?

Fear makes her hungry.

Wah Sun is a little out of the way but this is what she comes for: the menagerie of animals in aquariums and terrariums screening the kitchen from the rest of the establishment. An albino python that might as well be stuffed except for its resplendent fatness and its seemingly oiled skin. A baby crocodile, or maybe it's an alligator—and what is the difference between one and the other anyway? A large bayawak with carbuncled skin and a crested, thorny spine, blinking its disdainful eyes at the customers. And her favorite: a giant, very flat fish with seen-it-all eyes that reminds her of an aquatic basset hound. It's grayish-black, about the size of two large pancakes, and makes the most minimal motions with its dorsal fins to stay put in a private spot in the green water.

You'd think it'd be the young waiters she's bonded with on her frequent visits, but instead it's the oldest employee, a short, bald man who looks like a human relative of the fish. It's he who'd told her that the fish is an oscar, commonly found in Africa, though this one was caught in the Pacific, having strayed far from home. They're aquarium fish, but this one had spent years in another Ongpin restaurant where diners chose their food from display tanks. But no customer could stomach the fish's ugliness, and so the years passed and the fish got bigger and even less appetizing, until somehow it had ended up here in Wah Sun, one freak next to various others.

Here comes her duck-egg porridge decorated with scallions and burnt flakes of garlic on top. Now she is really famished. Outside it has begun to drizzle, and the quiet streets of seven p.m. Binondo will be ghostly by the time she is ready to go home.

You do not tell the men who you are.

You ask for the lights to be turned low or all the way down. And though you'd think this would be a giveaway, it also signals a becoming modesty. It can be used as a turn-on.

You insist that the men come to your place. This way, it's easier to control what she calls the "performance." That she lives in an out-of-the-way, mysterious place like Binondo can be both good and bad. Good: anonymity. Bad: the clients' suspicions of criminality that anonymity breeds.

Your outcall visits must only be to hotels, and in these hotels you must have a personal relationship with one of the staff, preferably a concierge, but you'll settle for a bellboy or a maid. You give these contacts a 20 percent tip for their troubles, which usually runs to four hundred pesos. Never, ever go to someone's home. The casualties: Nene from Tacloban; Aurora; Saltie. They had been made to forgo their usual precautions by either the promise of larger-than-normal fees or enticing photos of the men sent over e-mail. They'd been lured to apartments in various parts of Manila and had ended up dumped unceremoniously near estuaries of the Pasig, by the slums. Saltie's body had been not-so-cleanly severed along the waist. Her top half was found in Tondo and her bottom, from which her "thing" had been cut off, dug out of a dump by the squatter areas of Balut.

The best bet is to have the men passed on by your circle. These men having been vetted, the sex is more relaxed. Though you'd have to wonder, if these men are so great, why would they be passed along by the other girls? But sometimes the answer is very simple: these men want variety. Variety upon variety. They want as many girls as they can get.

To them, to everyone, you are a girl, as normal as any girl. To preserve your virginity you will only take it from behind. That way, too, the men don't have to wear condoms. There is no threat of pregnancy taking it from behind. And what man doesn't prefer to go condomless? Never mind AIDS or HIV. Safety among the girls of her circle is a wish and a prayer: at night you may court danger, but in the day you don't think about it.

This is another story about why she will only take it from behind: she is the pet mistress of someone high up in the Philippine government. This jealous man employs a private gynecologist whose job it is to inspect his stable: the women are to remain pure for him and only him. And after they have been deflowered, they are no longer of any interest to him. This man is a virgin fetishist, a blood fetishist. Far-fetched and long-winded for a cover story, she knows, but in fact a true story: there is such a man high up in the government and his cravenness is legendary. Rumors are that he will soon run for president.

Her jawline is soft and more than convincing, and that was true even before hormones. Every night she has to oil and massage her breasts, because even though they look terrific, they can feel hard to the touch and sometimes, when the weather gets cold, they tend to get stuck. Lesson: never buy anything Filipino. Always go abroad. Maybe her new breasts will be from Scandinavia. But Scandinavian tits—Denmark is best—have a price tag to match their quality. Though in that part of the world, the moralities are not so hypocritical.

Her nipples are sensitive, even more with her breasts. Why should this be a surprise to her? But even before she can think of new tits to replace her old-school silicone models, she has to take care of things down there. Finally. After eight years. After a series of psychiatric interviews to determine her "stability of mind," her "100 percent certainty." She is finally taking care of things down there. In three days, she is flying to Bangkok—a middle ground between quality and price, not the best but better than anything available in Manila, and certainly more afford-able than Europe; with a lenient psychiatric screening process that is widely considered no more than a formality—a joke, really. Nobody "interviewed" will ever be denied; at least nobody who is paying for Dr. Srichapan's services. Alicia had gone to Dr. Srichapan. Now, Alicia doesn't have to ask for the lights to be turned down. She can wear a bikini without much work. And according to her—the number one question from the girls—she has a range of feeling down there. She can let the men fuck both without condoms and without risk of pregnancy. The only gray area is whether to reveal her story to the men. Pro: full-op tranny fetishists are not uncommon, and they can be made to pay much, much more than those who are only paying for girls. Con: why bother going through all that work of transformation only to undo it by one slip of the tongue?

The doorbell rings and it's Peter, whom she's expecting, but not until nine. Peter who has agreed to four thousand pesos, start-ing with some wine and oil massage and ending with him in her mouth. No penetration. He'd agreed to a high fee because being turned down by Charmaine in the past made him want her even more. This is no tactic. Peter visits every month from sterile Sin-gapore, and each time he'd requested Charmaine through the circle, she was always booked. Tonight will be the culmination of many months of trying and hoping. Charmaine puts herself in Peter's shoes; and in touch with his excitement, she gets very excited herself as she walks to the door. She is going to be very stern with him. Pretend stern. Who knows, he may agree to another thousand pesos as punishment for being too early. Thank God she is naturally pretty and doesn't need much preparation on her face.

She opens the door but doesn't get the chance to say much. It's Peter, but it can't be Peter, because she has seen this Peter before, here in Manila, a Filipino, not Singaporean. All this happens in an instant. Because this Peter doesn't stay still long enough for her to ask him who he really is. He moves and, by moving, becomes the world. All the rage in the world, all those quick-glancing, suspicious eyes on the streets of Manila— especially when she's in full makeup and despite the fact that she is known as the most convincing girl in the whole circle; all those judgmental looks of a lifetime betraying fear of sex and of difference that can only be described as Catholic—all of it is contained in the four-point star of Peter's knuckles as they meet her face, quickly turning the room sunset-orange, then black.

Catholic. Catholic. Yes, she knows who he is.

She can't feel her face but she knows work was done while she was unconscious. There, finally—sensation in her left eye. She blinks once but the pain stops her. Tears cloud her vision. Tears not from emotion but from her eyes' irritation at some foreign substance. Maybe blood. Maybe bits from not-Peter's knuckles. She is more afraid of encountering her face in a mirror than she is of him. Where is he?

It's as if she's called him back into the room. He is so young. No more than thirty, she would guess. He sees that she's awake. She sees the knife in his hands. The blade is glistening. She thinks to inspect herself down there but stops herself. If she can't feel anything, then it's not real. Not yet.

Then she sees his left arm. He has rolled both shirtsleeves up and on his left arm he has made knife notches. Maybe the blood on the knife is his and not hers.

He starts to recite the Our Father.

Catholic. Catholic.

He is looking at her with fervor—as if she's Our Father and it's she who he's praying to.

Benjamin. That's his name. Son of Esmeralda, one of the Catholic matrons she's patronized. Esmeralda of Sampaloc. The son does not look like the mother. The mother has an ascetic face, very little makeup, which is unusual for someone of her class and of her Spanish mestizo background—above all else, for that type of woman, vanity and appearances. But Esmeralda has the certitude of God's approval and she wears this in the rigid stance of her shoulders, in the many disapproving lines on her forehead, the only blemish on her highborn face. Highborn, but fallen from grace, which explains why she'd resorted to reading God's wishes from a deck of playing cards for paying customers, most of them sinners like Charmaine. The son, on the other hand, has cheeks to which clings baby fat, even at thirty. There is something spoiled, something inbred in his appearance; the eyes too close together, the nose not so much aquiline like his mother's, but pinched, as if he's sniffing out something rotten.

Something rotten: that's her, face beaten to a pulp, oozing the garbage of a lifetime of sin. Now on to the Hail Mary. *Hail Mary full of grace the Lord is with you. Blessed are you among women.*

He kicks her. Pray, he orders.

She moves her lips, and a miracle: they cause her no pain! Though no sound comes from them, for the moment he's appeased. She keeps her lips in motion, pronouncing: *Fuck you, fuck you.* So strong is her will to live. Should this be a surprise? Her ticket to Bangkok, paid for in cash, sits under two layers of underclothing in the top drawer of her bedroom dresser. She can taste her new life in her rotting mouth, her tongue running into gum where teeth had previously been. She hadn't been entirely unconscious before, for flashes come at her now, fast and furious: Repent! he'd said at one point, before she blacked out. And then, she remembers waking up to see him crying, kneeling in front of her.

At one point he'd been shaking her awake, his face so tender and nervous, as if he hadn't counted on her being so weak, so easily extinguishable. She'd woken up, stayed awake for as along as she could, then blacked out again.

Now her nose is working and she can smell his pomade and she wants to puke. Then, mercifully, her nose is again stoppered. By blood, by a clot of disfigurement.

Glory be to the Father, to the Son, and to the Holy Spirit . . .

Even his hair smacks of Catholic repression. It's been plastered tight to the skull and parted in the middle, the pomade glistening in the lights of her bathroom. Tamped down, the wildness restrained. She turns her cheek to the tiled floor and is comforted by the utter coldness.

She understands now. The young-old boy Benjamin had been such a riveted skulker during her three sessions with Esmeralda. Charmaine had always thought he was sexually attracted to her but was afraid of his mother and didn't dare come close. Still, he'd wanted Charmaine to know of his attraction, wanted her to feel his presence as his mother had hold of Charmaine's palm, into which would be dropped the pertinent playing card, each number its own message from God. Which was the card for the Angel of Death? Had the Angel of Death ever made an appearance in any of her readings? Not just with Esmeralda, but with seemingly every existing seer in Manila?

She thinks back to Ah-ma's words: *Everything will be fine.*

What a fraud. Everyone's a fraud. Including herself, including this *bakla*-hating Catholic boy with the knife, who needs only to give in to his desires to be cured, to be freed. The knife is the penis he can use, she thinks, before passing out again.

Is she still alive? Why is she still alive? This time she tries to look down between her legs. She can't make out anything. She can't feel anything. Maybe she's in shock. But she's not wet, no signal of bloodletting. Maybe he wants her to be awake as he's doing it.

But of course it's him. She understands even more now. The bigger picture. God's-eye view.

Nene from Tacloban. Aurora. Saltie. They too had gone to Esmeralda. Like her, they too had wanted to stay on the right side of fate. Esmeralda the card-reader, the fortune-teller, the ex-socialite-in-hiding-in-Sampaloc, was one of God's chosen ones, with the power to sanctify lives by pronouncing positive messages from aces and spades and kings and queens. And in their turn, Nene, Aurora, and Saltie too, like Charmaine, had probably flirted with the boy Benjamin, who skulked when Nene was around consulting with Esmeralda, who skulked when Aurora was around, who skulked when Saltie was around, irresistibly drawn and, as is clear now, repulsed. Riveted by repulsion. None of those girls were as convincingly feminine as Charmaine. Maybe that's why it took Benjamin so long to find her. To find her out. He couldn't be entirely sure. What was the giveaway? A few seconds passing beneath an unforgiving streetlamp to reveal a not-quite-girlish cast of the jaws, the hint of an Adam's apple? A particularly tight pair of pants that highlighted a boy's narrow hips? Or did his mother Esmeralda tell him that Charmaine was a friend of the murdered girls, and by friend he finally understood that they were part of the same problem? He sought them out, Nene and Aurora and Saltie. He lured them to places where he could do with them as he wanted without being seen. Hadn't Esmeralda said that her no-good husband, the boy's absentee father, was a manager for a real estate company? So many empty units at Benjamin's disposal. *For* disposal. For his Catholic hatred and his ceremonies of proximity to the divine. *Our Father who art in Heaven hallowed be Thy name.*

Hallowed. Hollowed. Helloed. Fuck, it hurts to laugh. Even the rumble-beginnings of a laugh feel like a tremor in her guts, letting her know that parts of her are no longer connected to the rest.

There is a commotion at the door.

It's his partner. But of course he has a partner. To cut up those women. To heft those corpses—she's heard that death weighs a body down, doubling the living weight. To dump them from a moving car, as is the current police theory. All that requires two sets of hands. Maybe it's his mother. Maybe it's his father.

But then, silence.

No partner.

No second party.

No new pair of footsteps. Just Benjamin's, pacing, accompaniment to his never-ending prayers. *Oh Lord show me the strength to show my love for You, Oh Lord show me the strength to show my love for You, Oh Lord . . .*

No. This boy has the strength to do the killing, cutting, dumping all by himself. He has *fervor*. And it's fervor that got the pyramids built, all those stones made light and put into place by nothing more than fervor.

Fuck. Now she knows. The man at the door. It's Peter. The real Peter from Singapore. Benjamin sent him away. Peter frustrated by Charmaine's eternal unavailability. Poor Peter. Maybe next time he'll be willing to pay ten thousand pesos, so huge has his appetite for Charmaine become, so constant his frustration. If there is a next time.

Benjamin comes to her. Are you sorry? he asks. But if he'd only given her time to respond, she would've said yes, played along to satisfy him. Instead, no sooner had the question been fired than the right hand bunches into a fist, and if she has any teeth left, she is sure they have been sacrificed too in this new attack.

Albino python.

Python handbag.

Oscar. Like that fish, she too is barely alive. If she keeps to within a centimeter on both sides of her, like that fish in its selected spot, she can live on in the state she is for years, for decades. No teeth, no problem. Busted face, flies laying eggs in the crevices of her exposed flesh, no problem. She has heard of maggots eating away putrefaction, curing disease.

She is sure her eyes are as orbed and as dead as the bayawak's.

She hears him come back into the room. Why isn't she dead? What is he keeping her alive for? She pretends to lie lifeless. Now she remembers: an alligator has a longer, thinner snout of a face than a crocodile.

She feels him drag her body into the living room.

Nene was formerly Nestor.

Aurora, Esteban.

Saltie, Orville.

And she? She was once Norma. Norma from Norman, a long-despised name from an ill-fitting childhood. Catholic school, check. Catholic Mass every Sunday, check. Parents ashamed of his self-revelation, check. Self-revelation turned to self-disgust, check. Not until he was Norma did he feel even half-alive. And then that pleasure was taken from her by the club sobriquet: *Normal Norma*. Who'd started calling her that, intending it as a tribute, intending to make her feel comfortable in her new life? No, not normal, that's not the way she felt. Extraordinary, not normal at all. So she changed her name once more. Moving up from normal. Charmaine from a magazine. A model's name. A model, with that bounce, that self-confidence, that earning capacity. Charmaine.

She tastes blood in her mouth. She lets it pool, then opens her lips to let the whole thing, saliva and all, dribble away. She feels something hard slide along with it. Her teeth.

The ticket to Bangkok is made out to Norman. To match her passport. Her application form to Dr. Srichapan: *Norman*.

Norman. Norma. Charmaine.

Charmaine still.

On and on he is dragging her. Does he think she is dead? She can't feel the area between her legs. At least, she no longer has to go to Bangkok. If he's already done it. Like he did to Saltie. Saltie's "thing" never found.

He probably threw it into the Pasig River, let the fish have it.

She lets her hands relax and open, surrendering to her fate. The fight has gone out of her finally, after how many hours? Her arms are bumped along by the motion of his dragging. And her hands acquaint themselves, floor-level, with the objects of her well-curated home: the base of a lamp, a leg of her leather couch, the felt-covered base of one of the chrome legs of her glass-topped coffee table. It's her place of business, after all, not just her home, and has been furnished according to some idea of a bachelor's private space, she being the prime decor in this gentleman's haven. Nobody stepping off the streets of Binondo could imagine this plush, private room waiting for them. This room and Charmaine.

A flash. Of. What is it? Survival instinct? Anger? A delayed neurological twitch begun by her not-quite-laugh, that tug in the gut? It spreads from her midsection, fanning upward as a wave of heat, to her breasts, to her neck, and outward toward her arms and hands, which flex and test their still-aliveness. Her right hand grabs at the nearest object, a large stone she uses to rest her phone on. It's smooth, there's nothing really to hold on to, but she does, a sliver of an edge, and to do so, she uses all her upper-body strength, everything in resistance to his force on her legs, which, in the same instant as her hand finds the rock, kick free.

When the villains in horror movies startle awake after having been beaten, knifed, torched, shot—she now understands this is exactly true to life. Some fight against death always remains. She joins her other hand to the rock. She lifts. She throws the heavy projectile at him. But the thing falls backward instead of flying at its intended target. He laughs. He is chuckling at her nerve. A crash behind her. It's the coffee table. She is sobbing at the futility of her last-ditch effort. She can't stand, her legs are like boneless things, or nerves have been severed and they are no longer commandable. Her torso collapses to the floor, she slithers away. He grabs her feet again, pulls her toward him. Where is the knife? If both hands are on her, what is he using to hold the blade? A man screams and it's only after a moment that she realizes it's her. Crying. Calling. In her wordless wail are contained so many prayers: Oh Bangkok. Oh new me. Oh a life anew. Oh a real girl, more real than any real girl.

Her torso shoots up, like a jack-in-the-box. It startles him. You fucking bitch! he says, involuntarily letting go of her legs, which smack the ground yet cause her no pain.

He moves around to try to take hold of her by the hair.

There is something in her right hand. A sliver of her broken coffee table. A shard. It feels so right sitting there, her grip on it so tight it draws her blood. Around he comes and up and then down goes her hand with the shard in it, into his shoes. He screams. She mumbles something, incomprehensible even to her, just air bubbles and liquid, her turn to pray.

Our Father who art in Heaven.

She takes the sliver out. She doesn't know how far in she's plunged. Despite his screams, she might only have broken skin. It's always this way with people who love inflicting physical damage—they themselves can't take even the slightest breach of their own bodies.

She slashes at his knee, then at the fist flying right at her face. She gets him in the knuckle, then in the face. Just slashes. No, actually, one of these slashes has begun to yield blood. Now she's unappeasable, with renewed energy. She flails with the shard. She gets scream upon scream. She slithers away from the stomp of his uninjured foot. She slithers away some more.

He comes toward her. You will regret this! She picks up bits of broken glass and showers him with them. He comes toward her again, mindful of the shard, dripping his blood and hers, con-joined, in her hands.

He feints. She falls for it. His fist finds the side of her head. She is crying. His other fist comes flying but she is ready. To move so close to her, he has made his face available—the closest its evil judgment has come to her. She finds an eye with the shard. It's luck but she has also put all her remaining concentration into that plunge. It slides in like a hot knife cutting a sliver of cake. He screams. She pulls it out and finds his open mouth, taking pieces of skin and gums and his tongue. Then she finds his throat and the sliver is stuck there, stopping all of his prayers, and then very quickly, his breath, and he is just another spent body lying next to her on the floor, wetted down not by semen but by blood, lots and lots of it.

* * *

How many hours? She'd blacked out, and coming to, she is surprised by the presence of his corpse, now cold. She is barely warmer than he. She spends countless minutes finding her cell phone, then countless more trying to make herself understood by post-op Alicia. Frustrated, she breaks down in sobs, and only then does the voice on the other end go, Charmaine? What's wrong?

She doesn't remember answering the door but how did Alicia get in? Alicia breaks down and Charmaine has to look away.

When Charmaine peers back, Alicia is taking her picture with a phone camera. The fucking bitch. But no words come out of Charmaine's mouth, just jumbled sounds that are meant to signal anger—and her face? How can anger form itself on her throbbing, altered features? Alicia takes another picture, then another.

Alicia leaves the room. In a moment, she returns to announce that having heard what had happened to Charmaine—Alicia had used the words "street beating" and "anonymous crime"—and with the pictures as proof, Dr. Srichapan's office would not, as is the usual policy, forfeit the security deposit for Charmaine's cancellation.

But now of course Charmaine would need other operations first.

And though Charmaine is grateful to Alicia for taking the initiative with Dr. Srichapan, she also knows that Alicia gets pleasure in having lasting proof of Charmaine's downfall, pleasure that Charmaine can no longer be the prettiest of their circle.

Six months in recovery and her healed face gives her an almost Chinese cast. She has continued eating at Wah Sun because they don't disturb her there. Alicia had called a friend and they had turned Charmaine's bathtub into a slaughterhouse, where Benjamin's body was cut up, desanguinated. With this friend, Alicia and also another girl, Beatrice, had disposed of the disparate parts, sealed in plastic garbage bags, in different parts of the city. Alicia would not tell her where. Except to say that the head and hands, markers of identity, were thrown into the Pasig, whose frequently stagnant waters likely sucked the bags down into its sediment.

The girls had pooled money for Charmaine's operation and physical therapy, and they had also donated a small living wage to help tide Charmaine through this unemployable stage. How Alicia has paid the butcher/helper who took care of Benjamin's body, Charmaine doesn't know and doesn't want to find out.

Seven months later, she goes to Ah-ma's. Ah-ma, who betrayed her. She forces the fat woman on her knees, having persuaded the grandson to go into another room and then locked the door behind him. She takes out a knife. She asks the Chinese woman to take a close look at her face. Why wasn't she warned? Charmaine could have taken measures. Ah-ma says the responsibility wasn't with her. After all, Charmaine and all clients ask the questions they want answered. And indeed, everything went all right with Charmaine. She survived.

She lived where others perished.

She triumphed.

And her face—Ah-ma can't help but observe how much more feminine Charmaine is now: the jaw, the nose; softer, less sharp.

In the end, Charmaine can't make herself do it. So she asks the fat woman for money. All the money that she'd been paying over the last two years. Close to ten thousand pesos. A refund.

Upstairs in the squalor of her living quarters, the fat woman scrounges in cupboards, underneath the sofa cushions, beneath and behind the sofa. Charmaine can't believe the stench. She lives here with that grandson? Poor kid. Charmaine takes everything that Ah-ma can find—or so the woman claims. But Charmaine doesn't want to linger. She doesn't count the bills. Maybe half of what is owed to her. Probably less. The bills in the pockets of her skirt as she descends the creaky wooden stairs and out of Ah-ma's life forever make her look like a teddy bear with loose stuffing.

Alicia and Charmaine knock. Esmeralda answers the door and smiles at the two women. It's been a long time, Esmeralda says. Okay. The fortune-teller isn't shocked that Charmaine is still alive. That might be a sign that she knows nothing, that her son operated on his own. It may also be a sign of her acting gifts. Alicia looks behind her at the quiet residential street before both she and Charmaine disappear into the cool, shadowy interior of Esmeralda's Sampaloc home. In Alicia's purse there is a knife, and a cell phone with the butcher/helper's number. But first Charmaine must be sure. How can a mother not report a missing son? But that may not necessarily be an incontrovertible sign of guilt. To ascertain that, Charmaine will stare and stare into Esmerlda's eyes during their session. And if she finds proof there, she will act.

She and Alicia. Norma and Alicia. She has lost Charmaine in the attack. All she wants now is normalcy. But no forgiveness.

ABOUT THE CONTRIBUTORS

Viet Le

GINA APOSTOL was born in Manila and lives in New York City. She is a two-time winner of the Philippine National Book Award and has published three novels: *Bibliolepsy, The Revolution According to Raymundo Mata,* and *Gun Dealers' Daughter.* She has received fellowships from Civitella Ranieri, Phillips Exeter Academy, and Hawthornden Castle. Her stories have appeared in *Massachusetts Review, Gettysburg Review,* and *Charlie Chan Is Dead 2.*

Owee Salva

F.H. BATACAN is a Filipino journalist and crime fiction writer. She worked for nearly a decade in the Philippine intelligence community before moving into broadcast journalism. Her first novel, *Smaller and Smaller Circles,* won the Grand Prize for the English novel in the 1999 Palanca Awards, as well as the Manila Critics Circle National Book Award and the Madrigal-Gonzalez Best First Book Award. She recently finished a collection of short stories and is working on her second novel.

Antonio Adlawan

KAJO BALDISIMO'S artwork has been seen in the pages of Dark Horse Comics, a *Star Wars* comic book, as well as several magazines in the Philippines. While his day job keeps him drawing storyboards for Manila's top TV commercial directors, the most exciting part of the day (or night) for Baldisimo is the time he can go back to drawing the next page of *Trese.*

Wendell Capili

ROSARIO CRUZ-LUCERO writes historical and crime fiction. The sugar haciendas on her home island of Negros are her trove of materials for her stories of murder and mayhem. Although she has lived in Manila all her adult life, "A Human Right" is only her second story set in this city. Her latest book, published this year, is *La India, or Island of the Disappeared.*

Raymund Isaac

JOSE DALISAY has published more than twenty-five books of fiction and nonfiction. A Fulbright, Hawthornden, British Council, David T.K. Wong, Rockefeller, and Civitella Ranieri fellow, he teaches English at the University of the Philippines, where he also serves as director of the Institute of Creative Writing. His second novel, *Soledad's Sister,* was shortlisted for the inaugural Man Asian Literary Prize in 2007. He lives with his wife June in Diliman, Quezon City.

Marjorie Lachica.

LOURD DE VEYRA published his first novel, *Super Panalo Sounds!*, in 2011, along with his third collection of poems, *Insectissimo!*, following *Subterranean Thought Parade* and *Shadowboxing in Headphones*. He has won prizes from the Carlos Palanca Memorial Awards for Literature and the *Philippines Free Press*, and he won the very first NCCA Writers' Prize for poetry. He also fronts a spoken word jazz-rock band, Radioactive Sago Project. He currently works as news anchor for TV5.

ERIC GAMALINDA has published four novels, three books of poetry, and two collections of stories including *People Are Strange*, which was published by Black Lawrence Press in 2012. He teaches at the Center for the Study of Ethnicity and Race at Columbia University. Since 1994, he has lived in New York City.

Angel Velasco Shaw

JESSICA HAGEDORN was born in Manila and now lives in New York. A novelist, poet, and playwright, her published works include *Toxicology*, *Dream Jungle*, *The Gangster of Love*, *Danger and Beauty*, and *Dogeaters*, which was a finalist for the National Book Award in fiction. She also edited both volumes of the groundbreaking anthology *Charlie Chan Is Dead: An Anthology of Contemporary Asian American Fiction*. Visit her website at www.jessicahagedorn.net.

Mookie Katigbak-Lacuesta

ANGELO R. LACUESTA has received several awards for his short stories, including the Philippine Graphic/Fiction Award, the Palanca Memorial Award, and the N.V.M. Gonzalez Award. He has also been a literary editor of the *Philippines Free Press*. His short story collections have won the Madrigal-Gonzalez Best First Book Award and two Philippine National Book Awards. He is currently a private businessman and editor-at-large at *Esquire Philippines*.

Arnold Alderete

R. ZAMORA LINMARK is the author of *Drive-By Vigils* and two other poetry collections published by Hanging Loose Press, and two novels, *Leche* and *Rolling the R's*, the latter of which he adapted for the stage in 2008. He currently lives in Honolulu and Manila, where he was born.

Kathleen Hennessy

SABINA MURRAY grew up in Australia and the Philippines. She is the author of the novels *Forgery*, *A Carnivore's Inquiry*, and *Slow Burn*, and two story collections, the PEN/Faulkner Award–winning *The Caprices* and *Tales of the New World*. Her work is included in *The Norton Anthology of Short Fiction* and *Charlie Chan Is Dead 2*. She has received fellowships and awards from Harvard University, the Guggenheim Foundation, the NEA, and others, and teaches at UMass Amherst.

Budjette Tan

BUDJETTE TAN is a creative director by day, copywriter by night, comic book writer after midnight. He is the author of *Trese*, a series of urban fantasy graphic novels cocreated with Kajo Baldisimo. *Trese* won the Best Graphic Literature award at the 2009 and 2012 Philippine National Book Awards. Tan is also the editor of the graphic novels *Skyworld*, *The Filipino Heroes League*, *Bathala: Apokalypsis*, Erik Matti's *Tiktik: The Aswang Chronicles*, and coeditor of the YA magazine *Kwentillion*.

Tara Runyan

LYSLEY TENORIO is the author of the short story collection *Monstress*, and his stories have also appeared in the *Atlantic*, *Zoetrope: All-Story*, *Ploughshares*, *Manoa*, and the *Chicago Tribune*. A former Stegner Fellow at Stanford, he has received a Whiting Writers' Award and fellowships from the MacDowell Colony, Yaddo, and the NEA. He teaches at Saint Mary's College of California, and lives in San Francisco.

MARIANNE VILLANUEVA is a writer from the Philippines and the author of the short story collections *Ginseng and Other Tales from Manila*, *Mayor of the Roses*, and *The Lost Language*. Her work has appeared in the *Threepenny Review*, *ZYZZYVA*, the *New Orleans Review*, *Sou'wester*, *Prism International*, *Phoebe*, the *Asian American Literary Review*, *J Journal*, and many others. She lives in the San Francisco Bay Area and returns yearly to her father's home province, Negros Occidental.

NO AUTHOR PHOTO

JONAS VITMAN divides his time between Manila and Berlin. This is his first published story.